Nothing But Blue Skies

Dedication

For all of you with seeking hearts

"You will seek me and find me when you seek me with all your heart."

Jeremiah 29:13

Chapter One

Amber Wilson unpacked her suitcase, tossing dirty clothes into the laundry basket as if shooting free throws at a rapid pace. Everything smelled like camp. She'd had a great week. Somewhat disastrous, but still great.

Reaching for a sock that had fallen on the floor, she winced. Her shin still hurt from where she'd split it open two days ago while playing a night game. Thinking of the other mishaps that had plagued her throughout the week at high school camp, she sighed. Everyone had certainly seen the real Amber Wilson when she fell out of a canoe in the middle of the lake and when she fell on her face during the cabin skit. She'd known her week was destined to be disastrous when she spilled Pepsi on a cute guy the very first day.

But it hadn't all been bad. Her friend Stacey had asked Jesus into her life, she had been challenged to go deeper in her relationship with God, her counselor had encouraged her to be on staff next summer; And, she'd met Seth.

Amber reached into the pocket of her shorts and pulled out a folded piece of paper. Sitting on the edge of her bed, she read the words again Seth had written for her. She smiled several times at the sweet poem he'd given her this morning after breakfast. He had titled it, *This Girl Named Amber.* After reading the final line, she let her eyes return to one of the verses. The one that touched her heart more than any other:

But the time I'll remember most
Was at Fireside one night
I watched her praising God and thought
'She radiates His light'

She'd never had anyone write a poem for her before. Besides the warm-fuzzy feeling Seth's words gave her, she was also glad she had something tangible to remember him by. Otherwise, she might think she had dreamed her encounters with him, especially their canoe ride on the lake yesterday and when he'd said he had a desire to see her again soon--something he wanted enough to meet her parents this morning and ask for permission to come see her sometime.

"The washing machine is free if you have laundry to do," her mother said, peeking into her open doorway.

Amber folded the poem in her hands. "Thanks," she said, trying to decide where to put the poem for safekeeping. Her mother wasn't one to go snooping around her room, but she felt the need to put it somewhere her mom wouldn't stumble across it accidentally or toss it into the trash thinking it was garbage.

Her mom disappeared into the hall and descended the creaky wooden staircase. Amber rose from the bed, being careful to not put too much weight on her injured leg--another reminder of Seth. He had carried her to the nurse after finding her alone and hurt in the woods during a night game.

Stepping to the desk in the corner of her room, Amber placed the folded piece of paper on a box of stationery under its red satin ribbon. She would need Seth's address he had written down on the paper. She hadn't decided how long to wait before writing him.

Going to the computer and sending him an email right now, like she wanted to, seemed too hasty and pushy. She didn't want to scare him off. Hopefully he would write her in the next day or two and she could simply respond, instead of having to be the one to continue what *he* had started. This certainly wasn't anything she had initiated. If anything, her clumsiness and embarrassing moments should have scared him off already.

Amber put her empty suitcase away in her closet, took her shampoo, brush, and ponytail holders to the bathroom, then returned to grab the laundry basket. She had to walk carefully down the stairs and knew she couldn't too often for a few days until her leg stopped hurting so much. After starting a load of her dark clothing in the washing machine, she decided to call one of her friends she hadn't seen all week. Colleen answered on the second ring.

"Hi. I'm back."

"Hey! I got your letter. Did the rest of the week go any better?"

Amber laughed.

"Uh-oh. What else did you do?"

Amber filled her in on her other disasters. She decided not to tell her about Seth specifically.

"Did Stacey have a good time?"

Amber couldn't hold back a smile. "She knows Jesus now!"

"No way! Really? That is so cool!"

"I know. This morning before we left, she asked me more about how to know God. My counselor was right about waiting for that."

"Girl! That was so great you invited her to go with you. Is she going to start going to church with you too?"

"She told me she would. I hope she does. I guess I'll have to wait and see."

"I'll keep praying," Colleen said.

"Yeah. Pray for Kenny too."

"Stacey's boyfriend?"

"She's going to invite him to come with her tomorrow."

"I'll pray," Colleen repeated.

"Did anything exciting happen around here while I was gone?"

"Well, nothing compared to your week, but I did find a new job."

"No more working at Dairy Queen?"

"Nope. Safeway finally called me."

"Oh, cool. Will the hours be better?"

"The pay is--Oh, they're calling me right now, can you hold on a sec?"

"Sure."

While Amber waited, she wondered where her mom and dad had disappeared to. *They must be outside.* Walking to the back patio door, she peered into the backyard. The door of her dad's workshop was open--no surprise. He often spent Saturdays working on one project or another. Her mom was likely in her adjacent painting studio.

"Amber?"

"I'm here."

"I have to be at work in twenty minutes. Someone went home sick."

"All right. I'll see you when I see you. Call me when you can."

"Okay. Bye."

Amber had never had a friend like Colleen. They *always* got along. She couldn't recall ever being mad at her and was fairly certain the feeling was mutual. They had met in Spanish class last year when Colleen had transferred to Sandy High. By the end of the day, they discovered they had four classes together: Spanish, P.E., Biology, and Band. Colleen played the flute also and was seated beside her.

They were equally matched musically, but Colleen surpassed her in science and Spanish. Colleen had gotten straight A's all of last year. Amber's athletic skills balanced them out, however. Colleen couldn't play any sport to save her soul.

Amber hung up and was about to go out the back door to search for her mom when the phone rang. She wondered if it might be Colleen calling her back.

"Hello?"

"Hi, Amber. It's Stace. I need to talk to you."

"What's wrong?"

"My mom just got home, and we got into another fight."

"About what?"

"Joe. I told her I wasn't going to the wedding and if she marries him, I'm going to live with my dad."

"Wow," Amber stated.

Yesterday she had heard Stacey's opinion of her mom getting remarried. Amber knew Stacey had been hoping her parents would get back together, but she was pretty sure it was more than that. Stacey made it sound like Joe was abusive toward her mom.

"What am I going to do, Amber?"

Amber didn't know what to say. Stacey had come to her for help, but she had no idea how to handle this kind of situation. Stacey answered her own question.

"I think we should pray. That's why I wanted to talk to you. My mom has to get away from him. She can't marry him!"

Amber about fell off the stool she was sitting on. Sure Stacey had given her life to Jesus this morning, but to be the one to realize only God could handle this made Amber realize how quickly God had penetrated Stacey's heart.

"Do you want to come over?" Amber asked. Stacey had a car and her driver's license, but she had neither.

"Can I? Will you pray with me?"

"Sure."

"Okay, see you in five minutes."

Amber went out on the porch to wait for her. She thought again of the talk she'd had with Stacey by the lake at camp this morning. All of the prayers she had whispered for her over the last few years hadn't been in vain. Amber had always been open with Stacey about being a Christian, but she hadn't always known how to express her beliefs.

This week God had made it all come together. Now she hoped she could encourage Stacey in her new faith. *Whatever Stacey needs from me right now, God, help me to say the right words. I know I can always turn to you whenever I'm facing a problem. Help me to show Stacey she can do that too.*

Hearing Stacey's car coming up the driveway five minutes later, Amber waited for the yellow bubble to appear around the bend. Stacey seemed to be flying across the gravel faster than usual, and the car came to a stop behind the family van parked in the detached garage.

Amber waited on the steps. Stacey ran up the stairs and plopped down beside her. Amber had never seen Stacey like this. Her fearless, self-assured friend looked furious and scared to death at the same time. Without wasting any time, Amber took her friend's hand and prayed first. She honestly didn't know what would spill out of her mouth. She prayed for Stacey more than anything, asking God to give her peace and direction to know what to do. Inwardly she was also praying for herself, to know how to help her friend.

Much to Amber's surprise, Stacey prayed too. Since the first time Stacey had prayed out loud was this morning, Amber didn't know if her friend would feel comfortable doing so now, but Stacey didn't hold back.

"God, please get my mom away from Joe. She can't marry him. You can't let her! You have to do something. I'll leave the details up to you, but please don't let her do this."

Amber mumbled an 'amen' when Stacey finished, hoping God wouldn't let her friend down. There was no question as to what Stacey wanted. She had made that perfectly clear. But Amber knew there had been plenty of times God hadn't answered the way she hoped.

What if God didn't do as Stacey asked? Would she lose her faith in Him as quickly as she had gained it?

"Maybe I should call my dad," Stacey said. "He might be able to talk to her. They've actually been getting along pretty well lately. I know he doesn't like Joe."

"Do you think your mom would listen to him?"

"I don't know. She'll probably be even more mad at me, but at this point I don't care if she hates my guts. All I want is for her to get away from that creep. She has a huge bruise on her arm, Amber! Why would she defend him for that?"

Amber didn't know what to tell her, so she remained silent.

"I need to get home. I told my mom I was just going to the store. Thanks for praying with me. I feel better now."

Amber walked Stacey back to her car. "Are you still planning to come to church in the morning?"

"Yeah. I'll be there. I haven't talked to Kenny yet. I think his family might have gone to the beach this weekend. I'll try calling him later if I don't hear from him soon."

"Okay. See you tomorrow."
Stacey surprised her with a hug.
"Thanks, Amber. You're my hero!"

Chapter Two

"Is everything all right, Jewel?"

Amber looked up from her dinner plate. Her dad had noticed her silence.

"I have something on my mind."

"Anything you want to share?"

"Not really."

She saw her parents exchange glances and wanted to set them at ease without telling them the whole story. "Stacey is worried about her mom. I am too, I guess."

Her dad's face relaxed, and his gentle smile told her he understood. She knew her parents would pray for Stacey's mom, and she tried to leave the situation in God's hands, but she continued to feel anxious for how Stacey would deal with this.

"I know I've told you this before," she said when she had finished eating and rose from the table. "But I'm so glad you haven't gotten divorced."

"I'm rather glad myself," her dad replied. Amber saw him wink at her mom and lean over to give her a sweet kiss.

Oh, brother. What did I start? They'll be doing that the rest of the night.

After depositing her plate in the sink, she went back to the table to give them both a quick hug from behind. "I love you guys."

"We love you too," her dad replied, patting her arm and giving her a warm smile.

"I'll be in my room," she said, leaving them to enjoy the remainder of their dinner by themselves--and whatever else. They were always being lovey-dovey with each other as if they were the main characters in a romantic movie instead of her parents. But she didn't mind, she supposed. It was better than having them fight.

Once in her room, she took the book she had begun reading at the lake yesterday and stretched out on her bed to read more and get her mind off Stacey. After reading two chapters, she laid the book on her red and white quilt and put on some music. She didn't feel bored or restless, just thoughtful. It had been an amazing week. She'd learned a lot, and the camp speaker, her counselor, and Jesus had given her a lot to think about.

She did her best thinking here in her room. It was small, but she made the best of it. She also had a favorite spot down by the creek, but it was getting dark and too late to walk there now.

Her parents had bought this property near Mount Hood when she was three. At that time the house was a small cabin with a living room, a kitchen, and an open loft. She didn't remember it but had seen pictures of the tiny home before her dad expanded the living room and kitchen and added a large front porch, a master bedroom, and a separate garage. He had turned the original loft into two small bedrooms with a bathroom in between.

Amber went to her desk to grab her address book and transfer her new camp friends' information from her notebook. She usually wrote everyone at least once and then continued writing to those who wrote her back. Their house had an Internet connection, but it was very slow and couldn't handle much beyond basic email, so she wasn't on social network sites like a lot of her friends and cabin mates. If she was going to hear from any of them, they were going to have to either email her or write her an old-fashioned letter.

She decided to write a quick letter to her counselor, Tweety, thanking her for listening and encouraging her to apply to be on staff next summer. She also told her about Stacey's decision, and her mom, and asked her to pray for them.

Taking Seth's note from the box of stationery, she wrote down his home address, his email address, and his phone number, but she resisted the urge to write him. *No. I'll wait at least a week.*

Having a guy take interest in her was an extremely new experience. She'd never been on a date. And even with Seth she didn't know exactly what his intentions were. He'd met her mom and dad this morning before they left the camp and told them they could expect to see him again sometime, but he hadn't made any official plans to come see her.

All she knew at this point was he had been a very special part of her week. He had gone out of his way to talk to her and help her more than once. And he had been nothing but sweet every time.

Hearing a knock at the door, she looked up and saw her mom step into her room with a laundry basket in hand. The final load of her clothes had been neatly folded and placed on top of those she had already done.

"Thanks, Mom," she said, rising from her desk to take the basket from her.

"Are you sure you're okay, honey?"

She sighed. "I'm worried for Stacey."

"Not just her mom?"

"Yes. She was here this afternoon and wanted me to pray with her, and she asked God to stop her mom from marrying Joe."

Her mom didn't reply.

"What am I supposed to tell her, Mom? I've been praying for Stacey for so long and now she finally knows God, but what happens when her mom goes ahead and gets married and Stacey says, 'Why didn't God answer my prayers, Amber?'"

"What makes you think God won't answer?"

Amber stared at her mom. "Do you really think just because Stacey prayed for it not to happen that it won't? There have been plenty of times I've asked God for something that hasn't happened."

Her mom crossed the room to sit on the bed and invited her to join her. Amber sighed with the heavy burden she felt for her friend and for herself. She thought getting Stacey to believe in God was the hard part, but now she felt even more burdened.

"You don't need to be the one to prove God's faithfulness, Ammie. He's quite capable of doing that on His own."

Amber let her mother's words sink in a bit before responding. "But what if Stacey doesn't see it that way?"

"She might not, at least not right away, but God will be faithful to her and continue to draw her closer to Him, just the same as He does with you and me."

Amber still felt less than peaceful about the situation. Her mom tried again.

"Do you remember when your dad and I had the accident?"

"Yes," she replied.

"Well, we never really told you and Ben this, but we were facing some serious financial concerns then. We were thinking of selling the house, among other things, because of your dad's cut in pay at work. That's one of the reasons we went away that weekend, to talk about our options and make decisions.

"We had decided to sell this place, and the boat. And I was planning to get a full-time job for awhile. Then on the way home we were in the accident, and I remember waking up in the hospital and thinking: 'Our insurance only covers eighty-percent! Now what are we going to do? How could God let this happen to us now?'"

Amber felt amazed her mother had such thoughts about God. She always seemed so steady and sure in her faith. Her mother was constantly telling her, 'Don't worry, Ammie. God is in control.'

"But then when I heard your dad might not make it, I realized our financial concerns were so minor compared to that. During my days in the hospital, God kept telling me over and over: 'Don't worry, Carol. This is all a part of My plan. Just wait and see how I'm going to take care of everything.'

"Basically I had no other choice," she continued with a mild laugh. "I was lying in a hospital bed, facing the reality of becoming a widow with two children to support all on my own, and I gave it all to Jesus."

"So what happened?" Amber asked. "We're still here. We still have the boat. You never went to work."

Her mom smiled. "I guess God wanted to bless us, because that's exactly what He did. By the time your dad got out of the hospital, everything was taken care of. The church had that huge fundraiser for us, remember? Money poured in, covering the medical bills and leaving us with extra to stick away and help us through the next six months until your dad got his promotion and went back to getting his previous salary."

"So you're saying I should sit back and see what God does?"

"Yes."

Her mom gave her a hug before she left the room. Amber thought about what she had said and knew she was right, but it wasn't easy to believe right now. She felt alone in this and whispered a few more prayers, things she had already said but felt the need to say again.

She almost went downstairs to send Seth an email. He had told her last night he would pray for her, and he also knew about Stacey's new found faith, but she didn't know if sharing her concerns with him would be appropriate at this point.

The following morning Stacey came to church as promised, but Kenny wasn't with her. She said she hadn't been able to reach him yesterday and knew he must have gone camping with his family. Stacey seemed to enjoy the class time and worship service that followed in the main auditorium. She had to rush off afterwards to pick up her little sister and drive them to spend the afternoon with their dad. Amber didn't get a chance to ask her if anything else had happened with her mom or if she was planning to tell her dad about any of it.

On Sundays Amber's family usually went to see her grandparents. They lived in town. Her grandma always made a big afternoon meal, and Amber enjoyed seeing them today, especially since she hadn't been here last weekend because she had gone to camp.

Her grandmother asked about her week and fussed over her injured leg. "I have some ointment that would be good," she said, scurrying to the bathroom to grab a tube of something Amber had never heard of.

Amber rubbed the cream around her stitches, supposing her grandmother's remedy was harmless. She couldn't wait to get the stitches removed tomorrow. They were starting to itch.

"Tell her about your friend," her mom prompted her.

Amber told her grandparents about Stacey's decision. Grandma had to get a tissue to dry her eyes and blow her nose at the exciting news. Neither of her grandparents knew Stacey, but that didn't matter. Grandpa surprised her by rising from his chair at the table to give her a hug. He wasn't one to show affection much, although he was always kind and showed his love in other ways. He wasn't a big talker, making his words even more meaningful to her.

"God has used you to do something very special, Jewel. I'm sure He has many things to show you in the years to come."

"Thanks, Grandpa," she said, returning his gentle smile. "And thanks for all that praying I know you do for me."

He winked and turned back to his chair. "If there's one thing we can count on--God does answer."

Amber helped her grandma get the food on the table, and they all gathered around to enjoy the traditional meal of fried chicken, mashed potatoes with gravy, green beans, and fruit salad. The conversation never ceased, dancing from one topic to the next: everything from how her brother was doing and when he'd be coming home, to Amber's upcoming birthday in two weeks.

"Amber's planning to invite some friends to the lake on Saturday," her mom said, "and then we'll come here on Sunday and do family gifts then, if that's all right, Mom."

"That's fine," her grandmother replied. "I'll be sure and have a special dinner that day."

Amber looked at her mostly empty plate and thought, *Isn't that what we have here every Sunday?*

On the drive home later that afternoon, Amber's mom surprised her with a suggestion. "Maybe you should invite Seth to your birthday party."

"Seth?"

"Yes, you know that cute boy you met at camp?"

"Mom--" she whined. "I know who you're talking about, but don't you think that's a little soon to have him come see me? I don't want to make him uncomfortable."

Her mother laughed. "Somehow I don't think Seth would mind seeing you again so soon. I thought he made his wishes pretty clear yesterday."

Amber had a difficult time believing that. *Why me? He's got plenty of beautiful girls in his youth group to choose from. Surely he has better things to do on a Saturday than come to my silly birthday party. He might be the only guy there besides Dad and Ben, unless Kenny comes with Stacey. Seriously, Mom? Get real.*

Chapter Three

Amber tried not to get her hopes up about hearing from Seth anytime soon, but when she checked her email after they got home from her grandparents, she felt disappointed there was nothing from him. She didn't have much from anyone else either, and she felt a familiar frustration about not being more "connected" to her friends. In addition to not having reliable and fast access to the Internet out here in the forest, she also didn't have a cell phone. Her friends, and Seth, had other ways of contacting her certainly, but they had to go out of their way to do so, and she didn't seem to be worth the effort.

After a full week of camp where every hour of the day was structured and she'd had plenty to keep her busy, she felt restless and decided to call Colleen and tell her everything about her week, including Seth and her concerns for Stacey, but Colleen didn't answer her phone. Debating about what to do instead, she decided to watch T.V. with her dad. He usually only watched two things: sports, and nature documentaries. Tonight it was a baseball game between two teams she didn't know much about. She would rather play than watch others play, but her dad's company made up for her lack of interest. She wasn't surprised when he put his arm around her and drew her close to his side. He kissed the top of her head.

"It's good to have you home, Jewel. I'm not sure about you going away to camp for a whole summer."

This morning on the way to church she had told her parents her interest in being on staff at the camp next year. They hadn't seemed too surprised and sounded supportive. She knew neither of them would try to stop her from going.

"I'll miss you too, Daddy," she said.

"I suppose I can't keep you from going where God wants you," he said. "But I'll be sharing my opinion on the matter with Him over the next few months."

"Daddy," she laughed. "You want me to go too. You've been praying for me to follow Jesus and seek Him with all of my heart for as long as I can remember."

"Yes, but that was before you had a boyfriend. I specifically told God, 'No boyfriends until she's twenty-five.' I may have to remind Him of that one."

"Twenty-five! You and Mom started dating when you were seventeen and got married when you were twenty."

"This is not about your mother and me. This is about you."

"Well, I wouldn't say Seth is my boyfriend yet. So far our dates have consisted of a thirty-second disastrous conversation at Taco Bell, a twenty-minute dinner in a crowded cafeteria, a first-aid rescue, and a canoe ride. I'm not certain it's going to go any further than that."

"A canoe ride?"

Oops! I forgot I didn't tell them that yet.

"It was no big deal," she covered quickly.

"And what exactly did you do on this canoe ride?"

"Talked."

"For how long?"

She shrugged. "I don't know. An hour, maybe."

"An hour?"

She laughed. "Don't worry, Daddy. He stayed on his side of the boat."

"What do you know about him?"

He sounded serious and genuinely interested, so she told him as much as she could remember, which was surprisingly quite a bit. She hadn't realized how much Seth had told her in the short amount of time they'd spent together.

"You know what I can't figure out, Daddy?"

"What?"

"Why me? I spilled Pepsi on him. I made a complete fool of myself more than once. He had to carry me for a half-mile in the dark. I'm not half as pretty as some of the girls--"

"Whoa, wait a minute, Jewel."

She slowly lifted her eyes and met her dad's serious gaze.

"You are a very beautiful girl."

"Dad--. I know *you* think that, but I'm talking about guys my own age."

Her dad got up from the couch and went to get something from the bookshelf in the corner. Returning with her parents' high-school yearbook in hand, he flipped to the pages of color senior photos and pointed out her mother on the glossy page. Amber had seen the picture before but had never heard her dad's perspective on it.

"This is the girl I fell in love with when I was seventeen years old. Who does she remind you of?"

Amber hadn't seen the picture in awhile and didn't realize how much she was beginning to look like her mother had at that age--only one year older than she herself was now. She didn't speak her answer out loud. She didn't have to.

"I thought she was the most beautiful girl I had ever seen the first time I saw her. I guarantee you, Jewel, that boy would not have come to talk to your mother and me yesterday, or taken a girl on a canoe ride who had spilled Pepsi on him, if he didn't like what he sees."

Amber felt embarrassed to be talking with her dad about a boy, but her heart warmed at his words. She hadn't thought of her dad as being a teenager at one time, like Seth or other guys she went to school and church with--or her mother being a teenage girl like herself. Had her mom felt insecure and been shocked by a cute guy named Craig being interested in her--the same way she felt about Seth?

"Do you think Seth will like it if I ask him to come to my birthday party? I mean, would you have wanted Mom to ask you--even if you had just met her and lived an hour away?"

Her dad smiled. "I would have gone to the moon if she'd asked me to, Jewel."

Amber laughed and gave her dad a hug. "I love you, Daddy. I think I have an email to write."

Going back to the computer, Amber decided to write to Seth while she felt bold. If she waited until tomorrow, she'd probably chicken-out. A short message flowed onto the computer screen much easier than she anticipated. After a few minor revisions, she read through it one final time:

Hi, Seth. I hope you were serious about me writing you, because as you can see--I am. Thanks again for the poem you wrote for me. What you said about me shining God's light meant a lot, and I want you to know I think the same thing about you. I'll never forget how sweet and forgiving you were about the Pepsi incident. You could have gotten mad or made me feel really stupid, but you didn't. And that's just one of the many ways I saw Jesus in you throughout the week.

Anyway, the main reason I'm writing to you is because I want to invite you to my birthday party on the 31st. We'll be going to the lake to swim and take the boats out and then have a barbecue dinner. I'm not sure if there will be any other guys there besides my dad and my brother. Kenny (Stacey's boyfriend) might be and a couple of my guy-friends from youth group, but since it's Labor Day Weekend I'm not anticipating a huge turnout. But if you can make it, I'd love to see you. If not--no big deal. Please don't change any plans you already have on my account.

Love,
Amber

She sent the message and tried not to worry about Seth's reaction to hearing from her so soon or how she would react if he said he didn't want to come. Trying to remember what her dad had said, she decided to remain optimistic until she had a reason to be otherwise.

She finished watching the game with her dad and then they had a light dinner. None of them ever felt like eating much on Sunday evenings after her grandmother's lunch-feast. She went upstairs to her room after finishing her sandwich, put on some music, and picked up the book she'd started on Friday. She only had a few chapters left and finished by seven-thirty.

She thought Stacey might be home from her dad's by now and called to see how she was doing. No one answered at her house, and she thought about trying her cell phone, but she didn't like to interrupt people unless it was really necessary.

Going back downstairs, she went to the computer and checked her email one more time. Her heart leapt when she saw she had a message waiting, but it was from her brother, not Seth.

Hi, Amber. Thanks for your message. It was really great seeing you this week too. I talked to Tweety today, and she's really excited about the possibility of you being on staff next summer. I think that's totally awesome, and I agree with her 100 percent.

Great news about Stacey! I just have to say, you are so much more on top of it with God than I was at fifteen. I'm very proud to have you as my sister, and I'm looking forward to seeing you in another week.

Love you,
Benny

By nine o'clock Stacey hadn't called her back, and Amber decided to go to bed. She needed to catch up on her sleep from the week, and she had volleyball practice tomorrow morning. Crawling under the blankets, she laid there awake for a little while, praying for Stacey and her mom, for Ben and her own mom and dad, for Jessica and Chantel--two girls she'd had in her cabin, and for Seth. She prayed his relationship with Jesus would continue to grow, as he had asked her to do. They had both prayed that for themselves at campfire on Friday night.

She also prayed for what might lie ahead in the future. If she and Seth ended up having a dating relationship, or if they just remained friends, she asked God to bless their time together and to help them keep it in perspective with the rest of their lives. She knew they were both young, with a lot of years to go before they would be ready for a serious relationship, but based on the times they'd had together, she had a special feeling about him and would be very surprised if their paths never crossed again.

Amber had dozed off when she heard the phone ring. Checking the clock and supposing her parents were still up, she didn't pick up the extension in her room, but a short time later her mom opened the door and peeked inside.

"You awake?"

"Yes."

"It's Stacey. Do you want to take it?"

"Sure," she said, sitting up to turn on her light and picking up the handset on her night table. Her mom left the room.

"Stacey?"

"Hi, Amber. Sorry to wake you. I just got home."

"Where were you?"

"At my dad's. This afternoon I told him I wanted to come live with him if my mom marries Joe. He and my mom got together for dinner to talk about it, and they were gone for three hours."

"How did it turn out?"

Stacey started crying.

"Stacey? What happened?" Amber asked, having no idea what to expect and fearing the worst.

"He got through to her, Ambs."

"Who?"

"My dad. He told her he was concerned about her getting into an abusive relationship, and my mom admitted Joe doesn't always treat her right."

"You're kidding."

"No. I'm not. She's not going to marry him!"

Amber was speechless. She had never experienced such an immediate, huge answer to prayer before. "That's great, Stace."

"There's more, Ambs."

"What?"

Stacey had to take a deep breath before speaking her next words. "My dad told my mom he still loves her. They might be getting back together."

Chapter Four

Amber waited until Tuesday evening before she emailed Seth again. He hadn't responded to her previous message, but she couldn't wait any longer to tell him about Stacey's parents.

She'd had volleyball practice this morning and then Stacey had come back to her house. Neither of her parents were home. Her dad was at work and her mom had gone into town to take her latest paintings to local galleries--something she did to bring in a little extra income for their family but mostly out of her love of painting.

Amber feared Stacey's mom had changed her mind about not marrying Joe, and that's why she was so anxious to talk to her, but Stacey quickly confirmed otherwise.

"My dad came over last night and was there when my mom told Joe their engagement was off and she couldn't see him anymore. My dad was afraid Joe might do something if it was just her, me, and my sister there, or if my mom went to his place."

"What did Joe say?"

"Not much. He called her a not-nice name and swore at my dad too. But then he left."

"Is your mom afraid he might come back when your dad isn't there?"

"Yes. Well, she didn't say that, but when my dad said he was spending the night, she didn't argue. He's sleeping on the couch, but he's planning to be there all week."

Amber smiled. "I've prayed for a lot of things in the past that I haven't gotten. I know God had different plans in mind, not that He was letting me down, but I'm really glad this isn't one of those times."

"You know what's funny?"

"What?"

"I've been praying for three years that my mom and dad would get back together because I knew they still loved each other. But for the last two months, all I've been praying about is for my mom to not marry Joe, and when we prayed for that the other day I felt like He was going to do it. I had no idea He would answer my other prayer at the same time. I had given up on that happening."

"God has a way of surprising us," she said, realizing the same was true for her. "For the last two years I've been praying that Spencer would ask me out--"

"That guy in your youth group?"

"Yes. The one who took Nicole to the prom this year. At the time I thought, 'Okay, God. That's pretty much a slap in the face!' But now I can see He has someone better in mind."

"Have you heard from Seth yet?"

"No," she wavered slightly.

"You should email him."

"I did, on Sunday. I invited him to my birthday party at the lake, but he hasn't written back."

Stacey shrugged. "Maybe he's not the type to check his messages every day."

"I know. I shouldn't get all weird about it--at least not yet. But this is a new thing for me, Stace. There's a part of me that doesn't quite believe it yet."

"Well, I believe it," Stacey assured her. "I think your guardian angel knocked over your Pepsi on purpose and let you trip over that rock in the woods."

Amber laughed. "So what about you and Kenny? Have you had a chance to talk to him yet?"

"Yes," Stacey said with a smile. "I saw him yesterday before he had to go to work."

"Did you give him the letter you wrote to him at camp?"

"Yes. He said he feels the same way. He doesn't have any intention of breaking up with me anytime soon, and he's happy to keep things the way they are between us."

"You mean about not having sex?"

"Yes. And I told him about wanting to go to church from now on and getting to know God and stuff, and he wants to come too. He used to go all the time with his grandparents. He knows about Jesus, he just hasn't been going for the last couple of years."

Amber felt amazed and speechless once again, but she knew she shouldn't. She had been praying for Stacey for as long as she could remember, waiting for the right opportunities to help her know God. For so many years it seemed like God wasn't answering her prayers, but now she could see all the pieces coming together at once.

She shared all that and more with Seth in her rather lengthy email. She hesitated a moment before clicking "send" but knew she couldn't keep all that to herself. She had to share it with someone who would understand her excitement, and she knew if anyone would, it would be Seth.

On Wednesday she called all of her friends from school and church she wanted to invite to the lake party next Saturday, and she was pleasantly surprised to hear most of them could come. Only a few were going to be out of town with their families for the holiday weekend. She wasn't the least bit disappointed when Spencer said he couldn't come because he had to work.

Since getting to know Seth, even with the limited amount of time they'd had together, she knew she had never been as comfortable with Spencer as she had with Seth. Spencer was good-looking and popular. She thought Seth was cute too, and he seemed to be well-liked by the others in his youth group, but he had taken the time to talk to her, something that Spencer rarely did even though she had known him forever.

That afternoon she finally heard from him, but not by email. A regular letter was delivered to the mailbox, and her dad brought it in with the rest of the mail when he came home from work. She was in the kitchen, helping her mom make homemade pizza when he held it in front of her face.

With her hands wet from placing diced-up tomatoes on the pizza, she couldn't snatch it from him like she wanted to. But her dad was sweet about it, kissing her on the cheek and saying he would leave it on the table for her.

Once she had finished with the pizza, she picked up the white envelope from the table and took it to her room. Opening the envelope with a mixture of excitement and fear coursing through her, she took out the folded paper and sat down on her bed to read the words. Even seeing his handwriting gave her a little thrill.

Dear Amber,

I hope this isn't too soon to write, but Saturday seems like a long time ago. You probably won't get this until Wednesday, but I'm actually writing this on Sunday night. We drove most of the day and arrived here with just enough time to set up our tents and have dinner before the sun went down. Did I tell you

I was going camping with my family? I can't remember. My dad likes to get away from it all when he goes on vacation. No phones, no computers, no electricity. I usually don't mind, but since I just got back from a week at camp and there's someone I'd really like to email, this trip may be a lot tougher than usual.

I'm sitting beside the fire right now, and I can't help but think of Friday night. Standing there with you at the end of that Fireside was like nothing I've ever experienced before, Amber. I hope you didn't feel like I was intruding on your space and your time with God. I wanted to come alongside you as a friend in that moment, not just as an excuse to hold your hand and be near you--although that was an added bonus. I had a feeling we were praying for the same thing about getting to know Jesus better, and I want you to know I have the same desire.

I hope it doesn't scare you for me to tell you this, but I know God intended for us to meet. I almost didn't go last week because one of my friends asked me to go on a rock-climbing trip with him, but I was already scheduled to go and I felt like God really wanted me at camp. Ultimately I followed His voice. Now I know why He was being so pushy!

Anyway, I enjoyed meeting you--a lot, and I hope you'll let me come see you once in a while. When is your first volleyball game? Any chance I could see you before that? If not, I guess I'll have to be patient. And just so you know, I don't do this every summer: meet a girl at camp, write her a poem on the last night, and then write a long letter the day after I get home. Other than a two-week romance in the sixth *grade, I haven't ever had a girlfriend, and I hadn't planned on dating until after high school. But from that moment I met you at Taco Bell, I haven't been able to get you out of my heart, and I miss you already.*

Seth

Amber read it twice, smiling more the second time through. Her worries vanished about him not being as interested as he seemed at camp. She wondered how long he was going to be gone and if he would be back before next weekend. Checking the postmark on the front of the envelope, she saw he was somewhere in Washington. She didn't recognize the name of the city and wondered if they were staying in one place or making a two-week loop around remote Northwest camping areas.

Feeling more at peace about the whole thing, she returned downstairs and set the table for dinner. Neither her mom nor dad inquired about the letter until they were all seated and enjoying their pizza. Her dad was curious about the Washington postmark, and she filled them in on that detail.

"Will he be back before your birthday?" her mom asked.

"I don't know. He didn't say." She went on to tell them about whom she had contacted today and how many said they could come.

"Are Stacey and Kenny coming?" her mom asked.

"Yes."

"I wonder if her dad would be willing to bring his rafts and canoe too? It sounds like we're going to have quite a few there."

"I'll have Stacey ask him," she said.

"I saw Colleen when I was at Safeway today. I didn't know she had gotten a job there."

"She just started. I'm not sure I'll be seeing much of her until school starts."

"Is she coming next Saturday?

"She's not sure. She's going to try to get it off."

Amber decided to mention something to her parents she had been thinking about since returning from camp. This summer she had gotten a job to earn extra money. It was the first real job she'd ever had, and she had enjoyed it for the most part. And earning her own money had been great.

"I was thinking of applying there too."

Both her mom and dad looked up, appearing surprised and somewhat concerned by her statement. "That's a big commitment," her dad stated. "You better do some serious praying about that."

Amber immediately realized she hadn't done so, but she wondered why her dad seemed against the idea. "A lot of my friends have jobs now."

"It's a big commitment," he restated. "Think about how busy your schedule gets once school starts, Jewel. And your junior year is certain to have more homework. If you get a job, something else is bound to suffer."

Amber knew he was right. She could barely keep up with her schoolwork as it was. The thought of being busier didn't sound appealing, but having a job this summer had made her feel more independent and grown-up. She felt like a baby not having a job when most of her friends did.

"Ben got a job when he was sixteen," she pressed further.

"Yes. Because he wanted to get a car," her mother said. "But once he saved enough and bought it, he couldn't quit because of gas and insurance. And that's why he ended up not playing baseball this spring and almost didn't go to camp this summer. If you want anyone's advice, Ammie, he'd be the one to ask."

Chapter Five

Over the next few days Amber did pray seriously about whether or not to get a job during the school year. She knew the extra money would be nice, but she also knew it would take up a lot of time she didn't have unless she gave up playing volleyball, something she had no desire to do.

She emailed Ben about it, and he confirmed what her parents had said about it being a big commitment and something that became hard to give up once he got started. The final words of his email summed up his opinion nicely:

Unless you feel God is telling you to get a job, I say don't. Spend time having fun with your friends and doing stuff you love. High school will be over before you know it.

She felt pretty certain God wasn't telling her to get a job. Her parents didn't expect her to. Other than having her own money to spend, she didn't have much reason to. And then on Wednesday of the following week--one week after first mentioning the possibility to her mom and dad, she got the ultimate confirmation about the way she was leaning.

She had received three more letters from Seth, and another arrived on Wednesday afternoon. She hadn't been able to write him and knew he hadn't read her emails yet, so he had no idea she had been thinking about the possibility of getting a job. The postmark on his letter had remained the same, so she knew they were staying in one place, but he still hadn't mentioned when he would be back.

Dear Amber,

I hope you're not tired of these silly letters. I keep telling myself to wait a few days until I have something significant to say, but then I end up sitting down by the fire and taking my notebook out. I find you very easy to write to. I hope you equally enjoy hearing from me. If not, sorry. I'll try to keep this one short.

Amber smiled, wondering what Seth considered to be a short letter. So far he hadn't been able to keep one to under a page. And this one had three pages. She felt a little disappointed when she found out they were planning to stay through the end of the week and return sometime late Saturday. He wouldn't be home in time to make it for her birthday. But if his eagerness to write to her was any indication of how much he would be making time to see her in the coming months, she supposed she could wait a few more days.

The final paragraphs of the letter caught her eye the most. She read them twice to make sure she hadn't imagined it:

I'd like you to pray for me about something, Amber. I've been struggling with this decision all summer, and my time is running out. In June I got a job, and it's a really good one. A man at my church has his own printing business, and I had been working full-time there up until the week I went to camp. He's giving me the option of working part-time when we get back from vacation (mostly after school and some Saturdays). I enjoy the work, and he's a great boss, and the pay is really nice, but I know this will cut into a lot of my time. I'm really feeling lost about what to do. I keep praying, but I don't feel like God is giving me clear direction. I'd appreciate any prayers you could whisper for me. One way I suppose this does affect you is I won't be able to see you as much if I end up working a lot of Saturdays, but on the other hand I won't have much money to spend on you if I don't have a job.

I hope you're having a great week. Hey, do me a favor. Send me your phone number in an email, and I'll call you when I get home. Any thoughts on when I can see you? I'll give you until Saturday night to have an answer for me.

Still missing you,
Seth

Amber didn't know what God had in mind for Seth concerning the job, but she did write him an email, sharing how she had spent the last week thinking about the same thing and the advice she had been given. One thing she did tell him concerning her opinion of him keeping the job was this:

Please don't decide to keep working just so you have money to spend on me. I'd be happy with a canoe ride any day :)

She also included her phone number and told him what time she expected to be home on Saturday evening. At this point she planned to say she would be happy to see him anytime: Sunday afternoon or Monday. Her first volleyball match was on Tuesday, and the following weekend would be fine too, although she hoped he wouldn't wait that long.

Ben came home that night. Camp had ended last week, and he'd been on the staff retreat over the weekend and then spent a few extra days camping with two of his friends. He appeared happy to be home, and Amber welcomed him with a big hug. She knew it would be tough saying good-bye to him again in another few weeks when he took off for college, but she tried not to think about that right now. They stayed up late talking, mostly about his summer at camp. He said this year had been especially good for him spiritually, and he felt more prepared for going away to school. He encouraged her to go next summer like she was planning.

"So what's this I hear about you meeting a guy at camp?" he finally got around to asking.

She filled him in on the basics. He laughed in all the appropriate places, but his concern about what kind of guy Seth was came through loud and clear also. She thought the best way to let him see for himself was to show him the poem Seth had written her. She hadn't let anyone else read it, but she felt comfortable sharing it with him.

"How old is he?" Ben asked when he finished. "The same age as you?"

"I think so. He's going to be a junior too."

"She radiates His light," Ben echoed the words of the poem. "I'd have to agree with that, Amber, and any guy who recognizes that about you must be all right."

"You'll like him," she said.

"Is he coming on Saturday?"

"He's on vacation with his family. They're not getting back until late that night. But I think you'll be meeting him very soon."

"Have you heard from him since camp?" She could hear the fear in her brother's voice that she was taking a poem and a few brief encounters too seriously.

She laughed. "Let's see, today I got letter number five."

"Okay. He's gone on you," he said, sitting forward and giving her a hug. "Make sure he treats you right, okay?"

"Okay," she said. Her brother's love and affection meant the world to her, and he'd always been very free in showing it. She was definitely going to miss him in the coming months.

On Saturday morning Amber and her mom went to the store to pick up some things for the party: Food for the barbecue, drinks, and a cake, among other things. Amber felt excited about the afternoon, hoping those who said they would come actually would. Many of them she had only seen sporadically this summer, and she knew it would be nice to be with all of them before school started next week.

At three o'clock they left for the lake. Her dad and Ben were in the truck with the canoe, a raft, and inner tubes in the back. She rode with her mom in the van that had all the food and party supplies. By the time her guests began to arrive, they had the boats in the water. Stacey's dad had agreed to bring his rafts and canoe also. The weather was absolutely perfect, nothing but blue skies, and getting into the water and swimming with her friends was fun and refreshing.

After about thirty minutes Amber got out of the water and sunned herself on the shore. Watching some of her friends going out in one of the canoes, she couldn't help but think of Seth. She had really started missing him the last few days. His letters were so sweet, and she felt anxious to see his face and hear his voice again. She felt both excited and nervous about him calling tonight.

"Ammie, can you come help me get the food ready?" she heard her mom ask from the picnic area behind her. She wanted to whine her way out of it. This was her birthday. Couldn't she be with her friends instead of helping with dinner? But she didn't want to act like that, so she agreed with more sweetness than she felt inside.

"I think I left the hamburger and hot dog buns in the van," her mom said. "Can you go get them for me, sweetie?"

Amber took the keys from her and headed for the parking area. The water had felt great. Its crispness was perfect for the hot day. She could already feel herself sweating once she arrived at the sun-baked parking lot.

She reached the van and hit the remote device to unlock the back hatch. Lifting it up, she saw the bag sitting in the back where her mom said it would be. She reached for it and heard a voice coming from the side at the same moment.

"Hey, birthday girl."

She turned toward the voice and froze in place. She couldn't move. She couldn't speak.

Seth smiled and closed the remaining distance between them. Kissing her on the cheek and remaining close to her side, he left her feeling completely surprised.

"Seth? What are you doing here?"

"You invited me, didn't you?"

"Yes," she laughed. "But I didn't think you were getting home until tonight."

He shrugged. "They were predicting a thunderstorm up there, so we came home a day early."

"How did you know where to find me?"

He smiled. "I called this morning when you were gone. I asked your dad to have you call me when you got home, but he had a better idea."

Amber didn't know if she felt more shocked Seth was standing here right now or by her dad's romantic scheme. "You're not serious."

"I don't know what you told your dad about me, but whatever it was--thanks. I never imagined our first conversation going so well."

She smiled and turned more to face him. "I only told him the truth," she said, surprising herself by initiating a hug. "I'm so glad you're here."

"I'm glad too," he said, holding her gently for a moment before stepping back and letting out a nervous sigh. "Until I got home last night and read your emails, I was afraid I might not ever see you again. I thought seven letters in two weeks might scare you away."

"Seven?"

"Have you gotten your mail yet today?"

She laughed. "No."

"By Tuesday it should be eight."

She laughed again, not believing this was happening. "It drove me crazy getting all those from you and not being able to write back! And no, you didn't tell me you were going camping with your family. I sat around for three days thinking you didn't want to hear from me!"

"It's a good thing I wrote you then, huh?"

"A very good thing. I would have been a complete mess by this weekend."

Seth sat down in the back of the van and took her hand, gently pulling her down beside him. Looking into his warm brown eyes, she felt like she was doing so for the very first time. Two weeks ago she had said good-bye to someone she barely knew. Sitting here now, she felt amazingly comfortable with him. His letters had made her feel like she'd spent more time with him than she actually had.

"I never officially asked you this," he said. "I know we just met and haven't spent much time together, but if you haven't figured it out yet, I really like you. I've never wanted to see anyone more than I wanted to see you today."

Amber felt her heart thumping in her chest. Nervously she spoke her own thoughts. "I really like you too, Seth. I loved your letters. I hope now that you're back, you'll still write me some."

"I will, and I'll come see you--a lot," he said. "If you want me to."

"I want you to," she said, smiling at him in a way she knew she had never smiled at anyone before.

Interlacing his fingers with hers, he got around to his question. "Will you be my girlfriend, Amber?"

"Okay."

Seth smiled in return and reached up, brushing a loose strand of hair away from her forehead. She had her wet hair in a ponytail and was wearing old shorts and a t-shirt over her bathing suit, but for the way Seth was looking at her, she may as well have been wearing her most perfect outfit and looking her best.

"May I kiss you, Amber?"

She drew in a deep breath. She couldn't imagine him actually kissing her, but she couldn't imagine telling him no either.

"Yes," she whispered.

Seth leaned toward her and kissed her lips softly. She closed her eyes and enjoyed the tender moment.

"Happy Birthday, Amber."

Chapter Six

Walking side by side, Amber and Seth returned to the picnic area with the bag of hamburger and hot dog buns. Amber's mom greeted them with a warm smile, and Amber got the feeling her mom had already said hello to Seth once today, but she did so again anyway.

"Hello, Mrs. Wilson," he replied. "Thanks for getting her to come over there. I'll never forget that moment."

Her mother glanced at her and winked. "Surprised her a little bit, did you?"

Amber shook her head and sat down at the table. "My own parents are tricking me. I thought I was too smart for this."

Seth sat beside her and asked her seriously, "How's your leg?"

"Much better," she said, placing her foot on the bench-space between them and letting him take a look. "It only hurts now if I bump it on something."

He gently ran his finger along the scar line. "And how often is that?"

Her mother laughed.

"Hey, I haven't had any major disasters for two weeks," she defended herself.

"I better watch out, then," he teased. "Your time is about up."

She smiled at him, feeling amazed they seemed to be picking up right where they'd left off at camp. He wasn't acting any different with her here than he had there, even with her mom standing close by.

"Have you been out on the lake today?"

"Just swimming," she said. "All the boats are out right now, but maybe we can go out later."

"I'd like that," he said, moving closer to her on the bench.

She was about to suggest they take a walk when she saw Stacey and Kenny coming from the swimming area. She couldn't help but notice neither of them seemed too surprised to see Seth either.

"You two knew about this?"

"Were you surprised, Ambs?" Stacey said, taking a seat across from them. "I would have loved to see the look on your face."

"Yeah, me too," she laughed, knowing Seth was the only one who had gotten that privilege.

"I think it was better than when she realized who had carried her to the nurse," Seth said.

Amber smiled. "And much better circumstances."

"Much better," he said, looking at her as if they were the only two sitting there--the way he had just before kissing her earlier. It sent a warm feeling to her heart.

They ended up sitting there talking with Stacey and Kenny, and with more of her friends as others came in from swimming and boating. Amber enjoyed introducing Seth to everyone, and he appeared comfortable at her side. He also met Ben for the first time--officially. They had already met at camp. Her brother was one of the lifeguards, and Seth had talked to him one afternoon while they were there. He was considering doing the same thing next summer.

By dinnertime Ben and Seth were acting like best buddies, and Amber began to wonder if she would have any more time with Seth to herself for the remainder of the day. They hadn't gone on a boat ride yet, and she didn't know how long he could stay.

But sitting there beside him during dinner, as if it was something they had done many times before, she realized she didn't need time alone with Seth to enjoy being with him. Seth was just Seth. At camp, here, just the two of them, or surrounded by family and friends; his presence thrilled her no matter where they were or what they were doing.

After dinner Amber blew out the candles on her birthday cake and opened her gifts. She got several gift cards and fun items like a Lava Lamp and glow-in-the-dark stars for the ceiling in her room. She thanked everyone sincerely and said the gifts weren't necessary. Just having everyone here would have been enough.

"Well, in that case," Stacey said, reaching for her envelope with a gift card from her and Kenny. "I'll just add to my own back-to-school wardrobe."

Amber slapped her hand playfully. "You will not!"

Everyone laughed and began to disperse from the tables. Many of her friends needed to get going, but others hung around. She continued to wonder how long Seth would stay, and if she would have the chance to go for a walk with him or out in a boat. She knew he would say yes to either, but she didn't want to abandon her other friends.

Much to her delight, as the others slowly left, Seth remained. Stacey and Kenny were the last ones to go and were helping Stacey's dad with loading the rafts when Seth finally spoke the words she had been tempted to speak several times but had hoped to hear from him.

"Would you like to go for a walk with me, Amber?"

"Yes," she said with a smile. Seeing her parents beginning to take things to the van, she didn't know how long of a walk this would turn out to be, but she would take what she could get.

Smiling at her and taking her hand, Seth led them toward the water. Neither of them spoke until they were on the path that went around the entire lake and were out of view of the others. Amber felt nervous suddenly, and she decided to let Seth take the lead here. Whatever he had in mind for their final minutes together was fine with her, although she did hope it didn't end too soon. Being alone with him brought a different set of feelings than she'd experienced while sitting beside him for the last couple of hours.

"I was planning on coming to see you tomorrow," Seth said. "But I'm glad we got home in time for me to come today instead."

"I'm glad too. I hope you didn't mind sharing the time with my friends."

He dropped her hand and slipped his arm around her waist, pulling her gently against him. "I didn't mind at all. You can tell a lot about a person by the friends they have--and by the way they treat those friends."

Amber hoped she had done okay in that department today. She felt like she had ignored some of her friends she normally would have spent more time with if Seth hadn't been here, although she had made a point to talk to everyone and let them know how glad she was they had come.

"I've heard your dad call you Jewel several times today," he commented. Amber had gotten so used to the name her dad had called her for as long as she could remember, she hadn't given it a second thought.

"Yeah, he calls me that," she said without embarrassment. She knew there were sillier nicknames to be called by family members.

"It fits," Seth said.

"You think?" she asked. "Sometimes I wonder if Broken-arm Girl or Watch-out! would be more appropriate."

He laughed and stopped walking. Turning to face her, Seth gave her that look again that made her heart stop. "You are definitely a treasure, Amber. Your friends think so. Your parents know it. And so do I."

She felt embarrassed by his words. "I already like you Seth, you don't have to--"

He stroked her cheek with his fingertips and silenced her with a gentle kiss. "It's the truth, Amber. Everyone but you sees it."

If this is a dream, 'Don't wake up. Don't wake up!'

"I have a gift for you," he said, stepping back and reaching into his pocket. "I thought you might rather have me give it to you when everyone else wasn't around."

"Seth, you just got back yesterday, you didn't have to--" She stopped when she saw him open his palm.

"I bought this at the camp store after I told you good-bye, hoping I'd have the chance to give it to you someday soon."

Gazing at the True-Love-Waits bracelet, she didn't know what to say. She had seen them at the camp store and thought they were really pretty, in addition to liking the meaning behind them of sexual purity.

"Will you wear it?" he asked.

Lifting her eyes to his, she felt shocked by his openness, but in a good way. Her silence appeared to make him nervous, however, and he started talking again before she had a chance to respond.

"I know we just started dating, but I don't think it's ever too soon to make a commitment to purity. That's what I want for us, Amber. And I want you to know that from the beginning."

She smiled at him. She had thought about buying one for herself or suspected her parents might at some point, but she'd never imagined Seth would think to do so.

"Yes, I'll wear it, Seth. Thank you."

He reached for her wrist and secured the bracelet around it. "I don't expect you to wear it all the time. I'm sure with sports and everything you'll want to keep it tucked safely away sometimes, but I'd like you to wear it whenever we spend time together. It will be a good reminder for me."

"Okay, I will," she said.

"You're the first girl I've ever kissed, Amber."

She smiled, finding that unbelievable. He seemed to know what he was doing, and she knew he wouldn't have trouble convincing any girl to let him do so.

"And you're the first boy to ever kiss me," she said and then laughed.

He seemed perplexed by her sudden outburst. She explained the humor of her statement. "I've been waiting for my first kiss and wondering if it was ever going to happen, and then at camp I talked to my counselor and found out she hadn't kissed a guy until she was nineteen, and so I decided I could be patient and wait."

He smiled. "And I told God when I went to camp this year I was going to focus completely on Him and not get caught up in the find-a-girl-at-camp game. Those never work out."

They both laughed.

Seth took her hand and began leading them back. "Is it all right if I drive you home?"

"Yes. Can you stay for a little while longer?"

"I think I could be persuaded to stay for another hour or so," he said.

She was amazed by how easy and right it felt to be with Seth like this. She wasn't sure what it was about him, but somehow he made her feel very safe and relaxed. They returned to the picnic area, and Seth asked her dad if it would be all right for him to drive her back. He opened the door for her when they reached his car, and she slipped into the front seat.

"This is nice," she commented. "Is it yours?"

"It's mine and Kerri's to share. Mom and Dad got a new car this year, so we get the old one."

"It doesn't look very old."

"It's not. I think my mom and dad are tired of being chauffeurs. One of the perks of being the youngest of five kids."

"Have you made a decision about the job yet?"

"Yes and no," he said, starting the motor and putting on his seat-belt. "I'm going to talk to Mr. Davidson about possibly working only a couple of afternoons a week instead of every day, and then some Saturdays too. If he can use me, then I probably will, but if he needs someone who can work more hours, I don't think I have that kind of time-- especially now."

She smiled. "I was serious about being happy with canoe rides."

"In that case, maybe I won't keep the job and use being broke as an excuse."

She laughed. "Fine with me."

"That's really something about Stacey and Kenny," he commented, making his way out of the parking area. "Are they going to be at church tomorrow?"

"That's what they said."

"One of the things I've been praying about during the last two weeks is that we would have another couple we could double-date with."

Amber felt amazed Seth had already been praying about this, but at the same time she didn't. She'd been doing the same thing.

"One of the things I've been praying for is that I'd have more time with Stacey, and having another couple to hang out with will be good for them too."

"Maybe next weekend we can work something out," he said.

Arriving back at the house, they helped her mom and dad with carrying in things from the van. Then they went outside and sat on the wooden porch-swing her dad had made. Seth commented on what a beautiful setting this must be to live in, and she agreed. She hadn't always felt that way about her remote mountain home surrounded by tall trees and twenty minutes away from the nearest large town, but it seemed absolutely perfect right now.

"I suppose my phone doesn't work here either," he said. He'd tried to call his parents from the lake to let them know he was staying longer, but he hadn't been able to get a signal.

"Nope," she replied. "Do you need to call? We do have a phone in the house--and even electricity," she teased him.

"No," he said. "I'm here to see you. Everyone else can wait."

"Some Saturday when we have more time we can hike down to the creek from here," she said. "I'll show you my favorite spot."

"That sounds a little risky," he said, glancing down at her leg.

"I've been hiking that trail since I was five," she laughed. "I think I know it pretty well by now."

They talked for a good half-hour and then fell silent. But it wasn't an uncomfortable silence like they had run out of things to say to each other. More like they enjoyed being together whether they were talking or being quiet.

When he pulled her close to him and gave her a gentle kiss, she knew he needed to go soon, but she didn't want him to. When he finally said so, she tried to act brave and remind herself she hadn't expected to see him today at all.

"Thanks for making my birthday so special," she said, walking with him down the stairs. "But next time, give me fair warning so I can at least brush my hair out or something."

"I might not recognize you without a ponytail."

She had to laugh. All those hours in front of a mirror trying to get a boy's attention, and Seth came along when that was the last thing on her mind--at camp and today.

He kissed her forehead. "You're beautiful, Amber. Just the way you are. If you want to fix your hair, fine. But I already see so much more than the style of your hair or how you look in certain clothes. I see your heart, and I like what I see."

Chapter Seven

Amber waved and watched Seth drive away from the house. Rounding the bend in the driveway, his car disappeared from sight, and Amber sat down on the steps. If she could live any day of her life over again, this would be the one, and she wouldn't change a thing about it.

After a few minutes of recalling all the pleasant moments of the day, she went inside and ascended the stairs to her room. Grabbing her journal from her desk, she sat down on the floor, leaned against her bed, and started writing. Other than mentioning their brief encounters at camp, she hadn't allowed herself to write about Seth yet. Even with all the letters she had received during the last two weeks, she hadn't been able to fully express her heart in words. Tonight she didn't hold back.

She included every detail, writing his exact words as best as she could remember and the way he had made her feel. At the end of three pages, she wrote out a short prayer:

God, please don't let anything spoil this. I feel like this is a dream. I feel like it's too perfect, and yet I know this is the kind of relationship I've been praying for. Am I what Seth has been praying for too? That seems crazy! He told me he thinks I'm beautiful. Me! Amber Kristine Wilson. A girl with

scraped up elbows and knees who would rather wear
a softball uniform than a bikini. This makes no sense!

She heard a soft knock on her door.

"Are you busy?" her mom asked.

"Not really," she said, closing her notebook and tucking her knees into her chest.

Her mom came to sit on the bed. "Did your time with Seth end all right?" she asked. "You sort of disappeared on us. Your dad's a little worried."

"I'm fine," she said, unable to hold back a smile. "Other than Seth leaving, this has been a perfect day."

Her mom reached for her wrist and admired the silver bracelet. "Did Seth give you this?" she asked.

"Yes," she whispered, lifting her eyes to her mother's and giving her a shy smile. "At the lake when we went for a walk."

Her mother smiled. Amber couldn't hold back.

"Mom! What is he doing?" She hesitated a moment before sharing the intimate details of their time together. "He kissed me today, and I'm the first girl he's ever kissed! Why me? I don't get it!"

Her mother lowered herself onto the floor beside her. "Amber, why do you like Seth?"

"What's not to like?" she laughed. "He's sweet and fun to be with. He makes me feel special and like he really wants to be with me too. He wants to know God the same way I want to. He's been praying for our relationship and already doing things to protect it. He bought this bracelet two weeks ago-- after he talked to you and Daddy on Saturday morning. How can this be happening--to me?"

"What do you mean? Why not you?"

"I'm nothing special! Just a plain, ordinary, accident-prone girl. What does he see in me?"

"I wouldn't agree with that description of yourself, Ammie. But even if I did, can you imagine Seth, with all those great qualities, going after a girl only based on the way she looks? Don't you think he's going to be looking a little deeper than that?"

"Yeah, I guess so. And that's what he told me. He said he sees my heart."

"The same way you see his. That's the basis for a real relationship, Ammie. It takes more than fixing your hair and wearing the right clothes to get the attention of the good ones. A lot of girls rely on their looks to attract guys, but you don't have to. You've got a beautiful heart to go with that beautiful smile."

Everything her mom was saying matched how Seth had acted toward her and the things he'd said to her in letters. And although she thought Seth was good-looking, that wasn't what appealed to her most about him now. She was attracted to his heart for God, the gentle and sweet way he treated her, and the way she simply enjoyed being with him.

"Amber, how do you think a plain girl with plain brown hair and plain brown eyes and no beauty-pageant trophies ever snagged a hunk of a guy like Craig Wilson--the handsome athlete who transferred to our high school my senior year? I was the ultimate Miss Nobody, let me tell you, and then before I knew what hit me, I was his date for the homecoming dance."

Amber smiled. "What was Daddy like at seventeen?"

Her mother didn't have to think twice about her response. "He was handsome, sweet, and caring. And he could always make me laugh. I'd say he was a lot like Seth."

***

"When do you have Chemistry?" Colleen asked.

Amber took a drink from her water bottle before responding. "After this." It was the first day of school, and she and Colleen were eating their lunch. Other than band, they didn't have any classes together this semester. They were both bummed about that.

They heard the bell ring and went to their shared locker to get what they needed for their afternoon classes and then Amber headed for Chemistry while Colleen went to History. Entering the room where she'd had freshman science two years ago, Amber found a seat at one of the lab tables and hoped to see some familiar faces join her. She had very few classes with any of her friends. She and Stacey had literature together before lunch, and she had seen a handful of familiar classmates throughout the day, but mostly she felt like she'd transferred to a new school. It was weird.

"Is this seat taken?" a guy she didn't recognize asked, coming to stand beside the stool next to her.

"No," she said, knowing if he took the spot and this teacher made an assigned-seating chart, this would be her lab partner for the semester.

He sat down and introduced himself. His name was Christian. She couldn't recall seeing him before. "Hi, my name's Amber," she replied. "Are you new?"

"Yeah. My family just moved here from Alaska."

"Did you like it up there?"

"I've lived there all my life," he said. "It's all I've ever known."

"I've lived here my whole life," she said in return. "I know what you mean."

When Mr. Dunn started class, he said he wouldn't make up a seating chart until the following day, giving them a chance to sit beside someone they would prefer to have as a lab partner for this term. A few people Amber knew were in this class, but no one she was especially good friends with.

The following day, she sat in the same place and Christian did also. He appeared to be the studious type, and she supposed he would be a good choice for a lab partner. Science wasn't her strength, so she could use all the help she could get.

They performed their first experiment on Friday, and her suspicions were confirmed. Even though it was a fairly simple experiment, Christian took it seriously--measuring everything just right and paying attention to other details, as well as explaining things as they went along, giving her a good understanding of what they were doing, something she often felt clueless about in science lab.

Last year she and Colleen had Biology together all year, and it had been wonderful. Colleen was a major science-type person and always knew what they were doing. Amber hadn't had to touch a piece of dead animal all year and mostly took down notes while Colleen did the work. She got the feeling it would be the same with Christian.

Thank you, God!

"Are you going to the football game tonight?" Christian asked her after class.

She grabbed her backpack and slung it over her shoulder on the way out of the classroom. "I'm in the marching band," she said.

"What instrument?"

"Flute."

"Do you play one of those little ones?"

"A piccolo? No," she laughed. "It hurts my lips, and I sound terrible. But my friend does."

"Are you going to the dance afterwards?"

"I don't go to dances," she said.

"Why not?"

"I'm not a great dancer," she said. But she was thinking: *I never get asked to dance by the guys I like. Why bother?*

"I'm not a great dancer either," he said. "We could be terrible together."

Amber looked at him. *Is he asking me out?* She thought Christian was very good looking. He had Native American features: warm tan skin, black hair, and a nice build.

"What do you say? Make an exception for me this time?"

She smiled at him. He was very sweet, and normally she would have accepted his invitation in a heartbeat. An invitation to a school dance from a nice, good-looking guy-- how long had she been waiting for that to happen?

"Thanks, but I'm dating someone right now."

He put his arm around her shoulder. "Why aren't you going to the dance with him?"

"He lives in Portland," she said, feeling her heart begin to race at his closeness.

He leaned down and whispered in her ear. "I won't tell if you won't."

Her smile faded. For one brief second she actually considered going. Just meeting Christian at a dance wouldn't be the same as actually going out with him, and it felt good to be asked for once.

"Sorry, I can't," she said, ducking under his arm and deciding to take a detour down the nearest hallway instead of continuing on with Christian in the direction of her next class. "See you on Monday."

She turned away and was halfway down the hall before she looked back to make sure Christian hadn't followed her. Stopping to lean against the wall, she let out the breath she'd been holding. She'd never had to do that before and felt her heart pounding wildly.

"Amber? Are you okay?"

Amber darted her eyes to see Stacey coming toward her from the opposite direction.

"Why are you standing there?"

Amber knew Stacey wasn't a big hugger, but she really needed one and clung to her friend, doing everything she could to not cry.

"Hey, what happened?" Stacey asked.

Amber felt foolish. Stacey probably thought she had received bad news or something, and she knew she wouldn't get away without telling her now. Stepping away, she rubbed her nose that had barely started to run and gave Stacey a little smile so she wouldn't be too worried about her.

"It's nothing," she said, hoping Stacey would let it go.

"Amber? Finding you crying in the hall isn't nothing."

"I wasn't crying," she laughed. "I was shocked and confused."

"About what?"

She sighed and told her everything.

"I almost told him yes. Why did I do that?"

"We all want people to like us, Ambs. It's just natural, don't worry about it."

"Maybe I'm not ready for this."

Stacey laughed. "So, what? You're going to tell Seth you can't see him anymore? I don't think he will take that very well."

"Stacey! I was this close to cheating on him!" she said, making a small space between her thumb and index finger.

"Amber. You were not," Stacey laughed. "You told the guy no. You're not going. And I know you well enough to know you would never actually do such a thing. Thinking about it and actually going through with it are two very different things."

"What if he asks me again?"

"He won't."

"How do you know?"

"Guys don't like to be rejected. He won't ask again, and even if he does, you can just say no again. And, if he won't leave you alone, ask him for his phone number and then give it to Seth and tell him someone's trying to move in on his territory. Guys never speak to me again after Kenny gets through with them."

Amber laughed. "Seth isn't quite as buff as Kenny."

"This guy doesn't know that."

Amber laughed again and felt better. She gave Stacey another hug. "Thanks. And if you ever hear me say I'm going to a dance, punch me."

"I'm not worried," she said, veering off into her classroom. "Are we still going to the river tomorrow?"

"That's the plan. I'll call you whenever Seth gets here."

"Okay. See you at practice."

Talking to Stacey made her feel better, but that evening before she left for the football game, she wrote Seth an email telling him about Christian. She didn't have much time between getting home from volleyball practice, eating dinner, and needing to get back to the school, but she didn't want to wait until later. She felt like she needed to say something to him about it, and she wanted to do so before she saw him tomorrow.

Dear Seth,

Something happened today I want you to know. I'm not sure why I feel the need to tell you this, I just do, and I hope you won't be mad. A guy asked me to go to the dance with him tonight, and that's the first time anyone besides you has ever asked me out. I told him no and that I have a boyfriend, but when he found out you don't live around here, he tried to get me to go with him anyway. The weird part is I almost said yes. I don't know why. I really like you Seth, and I consider what we have to be the kind of relationship where we're not dating other people, but I guess I wasn't prepared to turn someone down I normally would go out with if I wasn't already seeing you, because no one's ever asked me before!

I hope this doesn't upset you, and I'm not sure why I'm even telling you this, but I feel like I need to before I see you tomorrow. I'm really looking forward to it. I hope you know how much. I don't want anyone else, Seth. I'm very, very happy to be your girlfriend. But this may take some getting used to. You're changing my life. And I like that very much.

Miss you,
Amber

Biting her fingernails all through the game as she sat among the other band members that evening, she had a difficult time concentrating and almost messed up during the half-time show.

Why did I say anything? Seth never would have known if I wouldn't have told him! What was I thinking?

When she returned home, she checked to see if Seth had replied yet. She nervously retrieved the letter she saw waiting for her. Letting her eyes fall on his words, she read them with her heart thumping uncontrollably at first. The thought of him being hurt by what she said was overwhelming.

Hey, you. Thanks for sharing that. I'm not surprised someone else asked you out, and I fully expect this won't be the last time. One of the disadvantages of having a beautiful girlfriend :) This is new territory for me too, Amber. Don't worry about it. I really appreciate you telling me, and the important thing is you didn't go. I'm sure we'll both be facing a lot of things neither of us have had to deal with before, and our natural instinct may be the opposite of what is right. Let's commit to pray for each other, that we will make the right choices in those moments--when we're apart and when we're together, okay? I'm sure God will be faithful to help us.

I'm looking forward to tomorrow too. I'm thinking I'll be there around eleven. If that's too early (or too late) let me know. Whatever you want, sweetheart.

Missing you too,
Seth

Chapter Eight

Amber had been anxious to see Seth again all week, but on Saturday morning, after receiving his email last night and reading it once again shortly before eleven o'clock, she could barely stand to wait another second.

Going onto the porch, she sat down on the steps. It felt like another warm September day awaited them, and she was excited about meeting Stacey and Kenny in an hour. She knew the four of them were going to get along well, and she'd heard from Stacey this morning that both her dad *and* her mom were coming to drive the boat for them.

"How long has it been since they've done that together?" she asked Stacey over the phone.

"Not since my sister's birthday party last summer, and that was only because Chelsea begged them. This time it was my mom's idea."

Amber had been praying for Stacey's mom ever since camp, and for both of her parents since her mom had broke off her engagement with Joe, and Stacey's dad had been back home on a temporary basis.

Seth arrived five minutes early, and Amber felt nervous about seeing him. Last time he'd surprised her, and she hadn't had a chance to feel anxious, but her nerves had kicked in about twenty minutes ago and reached their peak as she waited for him to park the car and step out.

Rising from her perch on the steps, she smiled and walked toward him. She noticed he had on the t-shirt she had bought for him at camp. He had gotten his hair cut since last weekend. Meeting him a few paces from the bottom step, Amber felt her nerves melting away. Last weekend she had begun to feel at peace in his presence after the initial shock wore off, and those comfortable feelings surprised her once again.

Without so much as a word, Seth placed his fingertips under her chin and kissed her sweetly on the lips. His touch still felt new but familiar at the same time.

"You can't do that to me," he said.

"What?" she asked with a smile.

"Wear your hair like that."

She laughed. "You mean washed and brushed into place?"

A light gust of wind blew some of her loose brown hair across her face. Seth brushed it out of her eyes with his fingers. "Yeah. You can't do that," he said with a teasing smile.

She stepped back and gathered the soft strands into a ponytail, using her hand as a holder for now.

"Is this better?"

His unwavering gaze told her the answer. "Not much," he said, stepping forward and giving her another light kiss.

"I love that I can do that," he said.

And I love that you do.

She reached up and touched his short hair. "What's this?"

"That is my sister's fault. She said if I'm going to have a girlfriend, I need to start looking sixteen instead of twelve."

Amber laughed. His previous hairstyle had been somewhat junior-highish. "I like it very much," she said. "But you better be wearing a hat to school."

He kissed her again. "No worries, Amber."

"I'm not," she said, feeling her own guilt returning. "Thanks for understanding about yesterday. That was weird for me. I'm sorry I even--"

"Shh," he said, pressing his finger to her lips. "I've caught my own eyes wandering a few times this week, and I'm like, 'What am I doing thinking about her?'"

Amber felt a pang of fear surge through her. She was so insecure normally, let alone when she had a good-looking guy who could be stolen away from her in a heartbeat. He saw "those girls" all week, and then had to settle for her on Saturday.

Her dropped eyes gave her thoughts away.

"I know what you're thinking, and you can stop it right now. I'm not dating you because there's no one else, Amber. I'm with you because you're the one I want."

She had to say it. "Really?"

"Yes, really!" He laughed. "It takes a second for my eyes to wander. It's takes an hour for me to drive out here to see you!"

He slipped his arms around her waist and pulled her close to him. Holding her gently, he repeated himself. "You're the one I want, Amber. I wouldn't have wasted my first kiss on you if you weren't."

Amber heard the front door open behind them. She expected Seth to step away from her, but he didn't. Her mom came out and said a friendly hello to Seth, oblivious to the nature of the conversation they were having.

"I didn't hear you drive up. Did you just get here?"

"I've been here a few minutes," he said, turning to the side slightly but keeping his arm around her waist. "I had a welcoming committee."

Her mom laughed. "I'm sure you did. Sorry to interrupt, but there's a phone call for you, sweetie."

Amber stepped away from Seth and reached for the portable extension in her mom's hand. Taking it from her, she leaned against the railing and said hello.

"Hey, Amber it's me. Guess what?" Colleen sounded very excited.

"What?"

"I've got the afternoon off! I don't have to work until four-thirty. Do you want to do something?"

Amber thought she'd told Colleen Seth was coming today, but maybe she hadn't. "Seth is here," she said. "We're going water-skiing this afternoon with Stacey and Kenny."

"Oh yeah, I forgot. Never mind."

Amber glanced at Seth. She knew he wouldn't mind adding one more to their group.

"Come with us," she said.

"I don't think so. I'll see you--"

"Colleen, you're coming. We'll pick you up in an hour. Don't eat first."

She clicked off the phone before Colleen had a chance to reply. It rang ten seconds later. Amber hadn't bothered to lay it aside yet.

"I mean it," she said without giving Colleen a chance to identify herself.

"Amber, are you sure? I don't want to be a third-wheel."

"You're not a third-wheel, Colleen. You're my best friend I've barely seen all week. Besides, I want you to get to know Seth. You didn't get much of a chance last weekend."

"Okay, thanks. I'll be ready."

Seth had come over to sit on the steps while she was talking. Amber laid the phone down and sat beside him. She told him about Colleen joining them. He was fine with it just like she knew he would be.

"Hey, guess what?" she said, unable to contain her excitement. "Stacey called this morning to tell me her mom is coming today too and will bring lunch for us."

"Stacey's mom *and* dad are going to be there?"

She smiled. "Yes, and it was her mom's idea."

"Wow! You're like a miracle-magnet, sweetheart."

She held his gaze. His use of that word in his email had been one thing. Hearing it roll off his tongue so naturally was quite another.

"Seth?"

"Yes?"

"You're the one I want too. You're the one I've been praying for."

He pulled her close to him. She laid her head on his shoulder.

"Let's not mess this up then, okay?"

"Okay," she said. "I'll trust you if you trust me."

"I trust you, Amber," he said. "We'll figure our way through this one step at a time."

Chapter Nine

When Amber, Seth, and Colleen arrived at the river, Stacey and Kenny were waiting for them in the parking lot of the boat-launching area. They didn't have to wait long to find out why.

"We're hanging out over here while my mom and dad are yelling at each other," Stacey said, appearing close to tears.

Amber gave Stacey a hug. "What's going on?"

"My mom told my dad this morning that he doesn't need to stay at the house anymore. It's been almost three weeks, and Joe hasn't called or stopped by. My dad thinks Joe is watching the house and waiting for his truck to be gone. My mom says he's being stupid. Things have been going so well between them--"

Stacey couldn't finish, and Amber did the only thing she knew how to do. Steering Stacey away from the others, she began praying out loud as they walked around the parking area.

When she finished with her simple plea for God's help and intervention, Amber held Stacey for a long time. "Hang in there, Stace. Don't forget how all this got started. God knows what He's doing."

Stacey appeared to do her best to enjoy the day. Both of her parents were on the boat together all afternoon with the rest of them, but they weren't speaking to each other. All of them took their turn water skiing, and everyone seemed to have a good time, but an underlying tension remained.

"Okay, no more putting it off, Seth," Stacey said two hours into their time on the wide Columbia River. "Your turn."

"I'm not a great water skier," he said for about the third time. "I'm going to make a fool out of myself in front of my girlfriend who didn't tell me she was such a pro at this."

"Oh, and like I haven't made a complete idiot of myself in front of you?" Amber said. "Come on. Do as the woman says."

Seth appeared genuinely apprehensive about this, and within ten minutes Amber knew why. He couldn't get up on a pair of skis to save his soul.

"I thought you said you've done this before," she said to him from the back of the boat, doing her best to keep from laughing.

"I have--this! This is how far I get."

"Do you want to keep trying?" she asked seriously. "You don't have to."

He gave it a few more tries and managed to get up for about five seconds once, but after that he gave up. He climbed back into the boat, shivering like a Popsicle. She placed a warm towel around his shoulders and gave him a brief kiss.

"You're so brave," she said. "You'll make it next time."

"Oh, no," he said. "There's not going to be a next time, sweetheart. That's all you get."

She laughed and gave him another towel to dry his hair and wipe off his wet legs. Sitting down beside him in the seat directly behind where Stacey's dad was driving and her mom was sitting, Amber heard her dad say something.

"You remember the first time I tried to ski?"

"The first time, the second, the third..." Stacey's mom replied. "You never gave up though. All to impress my daddy."

"All to impress you," he corrected.

Amber glanced at Seth. He was listening too.

"Hey, Amber. Toss me that lifejacket," Stacey hollered from the back of the boat where she was getting ready to go into the water.

Amber tossed her the vest Seth had been wearing. She heard Stacey's dad speak again when she had settled back against the seat.

"Seems like yesterday," he said. "But now I can ski, and I don't have you."

"Mike, don't start--"

"You about ready, babe?" Stacey's dad hollered over his shoulder.

"Yeah," she called from the water. "Just a minute."

Her dad spoke quietly again to his ex-wife. "I said I'd go home tonight. Don't worry. I was just stating a fact."

Stacey began her run, and her parents' conversation ceased. Riding in the boat at the high speed across the water's surface, while Stacey showed off eight years of water-skiing skill, Seth removed his towel from his shoulders, put his t-shirt back on along with a standard orange lifejacket and then draped his arm around her.

Amber leaned into him and prayed silently--for Stacey's parents, for Stacey and Kenny, for herself and Seth. Why did life have to be so complicated? Why couldn't people just love each other and be happy instead of having all this drama and heartache? It made her wonder if she was ready to be dating, or if she ever would be. But she didn't feel like she could do anything to stop what was happening. Maybe if her relationship with Seth crashed and burned soon, she would think twice about ever doing this again.

Colleen needed to be home by three-thirty. After Stacey finished, they headed back to shore. Amber and Seth drove Colleen home, then went back to her house to take showers and change clothes. They were planning to meet Stacey and Kenny in another hour, go out for pizza with them, and maybe catch a movie depending on time and how Stacey was feeling. Amber had told her to call if she didn't feel like going.

While Seth was taking a shower, Amber told her mom and dad about what had happened with Stacey's parents. They were disappointed at the news but not surprised.

"It could happen, Ammie, but not necessarily overnight. Stacey's mom probably needs some time. Last weekend she was supposed to marry someone else. Even if the breakup was a good thing, it's still hard."

When Seth returned to the room, Amber smiled at him just because, but he interpreted it as something else.

"Were you telling them how pathetic I was?"

"No," she said. "I would never do such a thing."

"But you would think it."

She smiled. "You tried hard--more times than I would if I was that--water-ski challenged."

"Pathetic," he said, sitting beside her on the couch. "The word is pathetic, sweetheart. It's okay, you can say it."

Amber glanced at her mother and smiled--not at Seth's opinion of his water-skiing efforts, but at the use of that word again. She wasn't used to hearing it herself, let alone having him use it right in front of her parents.

When Stacey hadn't called by five, they headed over to her house as planned. Amber had put on her silver purity bracelet, and Seth noticed on the short drive.

"Am I doing okay, Amber? I haven't done anything that's made you uncomfortable, have I? Even a little bit?"

"No, Seth. You haven't," she said. She had been thoroughly enjoying all the little touches and light kisses, and was surprised at how quickly she was becoming used to them. Seth made everything easy and comfortable--like she could simply be herself and enjoy their time together, rather than having to second-guess every word she spoke--the way she usually felt around guys she wanted to impress.

"You'll tell me if I cross the line, even a little?" he asked.

She knew she should say yes, but she wasn't certain she knew what the line was. So far she had been fine with everything and knew there were some definite things they shouldn't be doing, but what about all the little things in between--would she know when they were heading down a dangerous path? Would she want to tell him to back off, or would she be enjoying it too much to think it might not be right?

"Take the next left," she said, directing him to Stacey's house instead of answering him. He turned onto Stacey's street, and she pointed out the pale yellow house at the bottom of the hill. Seth pulled into the driveway and turned off the motor, but he didn't get out of the car.

Turning to face her, he reached for her hand and intertwined his fingers with hers. "You didn't answer me," he said.

She looked into his concerned eyes and said what she was thinking. "I'm not sure I'll know if you cross the line."

He gently touched the side of her hair. "I will," he said. "I'll be very careful, Amber. I pray about it constantly. But if I do something that makes you uncomfortable--even a little bit--just say so, okay?"

"Okay," she said, giving him a little smile. "I really like your hugs. You can give me one of those anytime."

He smiled and kissed her fingers before opening his door and getting out of the car. Stepping around to her side, he pulled her close to him and wrapped his arms around her, holding her with strength and tenderness.

"I like holding you, Amber. Thanks for telling me you like it too. I could do this all day."

She enjoyed the extended embrace, feeling amazed once again at how easy being with Seth was, and she couldn't help but think God had something to do with that. She remembered feeling the same way when she had helped Stacey to pray on the final day of camp. And she knew why-- God was there making it all come together at just the right time.

She knew He was here right now too. He had brought her and Seth together, she felt certain. She could feel His peace and approval surrounding them. She couldn't describe it to anyone else, but she knew it was real. And she knew all they could do was cling to Jesus and trust Him to help them on this uncertain, unpredictable, scary path that was absolutely thrilling her at the same time.

Seth released her, and they stepped toward the house. Amber noticed Mr. Collins' truck was gone, and a familiar sadness swept through her. She could remember when Stacey's parents were still married and all of them lived in this house together. Stacey's mom and dad had always seemed happy. She never heard them fight when she spent time at Stacey's house. Hearing they were getting a divorce had been a big shock for her.

Amber rang the doorbell and waited beside Seth for someone to appear. Stacey did within moments with a big smile on her face. Amber felt surprised by that and the hug her friend gave her.

"Sorry, Seth," Stacey said. "Didn't mean to intrude on your space there, but I have awesome news. You are not going to believe this!"

"What?" Amber asked, following Stacey inside. "I see your dad's truck is gone."

"Yeah, I know. So is my mom."

"Where are they?"

"My dad has this theory that Joe is waiting for a time when he's not here to come back and try to talk to my mom. And when we got back, my dad put the boat away and then was going to leave like my mom wanted. But at the last second, my mom went out to stop him from going and said she was willing to test out his suspicions. So she followed him in her car and they're leaving his truck in a parking lot instead of it sitting here like a red flag. He's going to be here for a few more days, but Joe won't know it."

"And that was your mom's idea?"

"Yes! And she wasn't being sarcastic about it or like she's trying to prove him wrong. She honestly doesn't want him to go--I just know it!"

Amber gave Stacey another hug and hoped she was right. She promised her she would keep praying.

"I'm going to try to talk them into coming to church tomorrow," she went on, sounding fearless. "They both need God, that's for sure. Even if they get back together on their own, it will never be all it could be. I figure I might as well start bugging them now."

Amber admired her friend's courage and tenaciousness. Stacey had always been that way about everything else: fearless and daring. She knew it shouldn't surprise her to see her be that way about getting her parents back together when she'd been given a small ray of hope.

The four of them left for town, had pizza at the place where Stacey worked several nights each week, and then went to see a movie at the theater. Seth and Kenny let her and Stacey pick. When Kenny and Seth left her and Stacey sitting in the seats to go get popcorn and drinks, Stacey voiced something she had obviously been thinking all day.

"You two are adorable together, Amber."

"You think?"

"Absolutely. You act like you've been together for a long time. I can't believe this is a first relationship for both of you. It's taken me and Kenny a year to get where you two already are."

"What makes you think that?"

"At first Kenny and I were very superficial with each other. When we went out, it was about two things: impressing other people we were with the other person, and letting our hormones have free reign in a parked car. I didn't even really begin to get to know him until about four months ago when I realized there had to be more to a relationship than making out and wearing his letterman jacket."

"What changed?"

"One night we drove to the lake like usual, and I told him that instead of kissing--and doing just about everything besides actually having sex, that I wanted to talk. I said I felt like we didn't even know each other, and I was really surprised, but he agreed. And so we did, and two hours later he drove me home and gave me a really sweet kiss at the door. I went to bed thinking, 'That's the best date I've ever had!'"

"And that wasn't the only time you did that?"

"The first of many. And let me tell you, Ambs, it's way better."

Amber told Stacey about the bracelet Seth had given her. She'd had it on all evening, but she hadn't said Seth had given it to her or what it meant.

"That's very cool, Amber."

Amber decided to ask Stacey about what she had been thinking earlier when she and Seth had talked about their physical relationship. "How do you know where to draw the line?"

"You'll know, Amber. Believe me. I knew before, and I've really known since we got back from camp. Go with your gut. More isn't better. It's just more."

Chapter Ten

Saying good-bye to Seth that night was much more difficult than Amber anticipated. Last Saturday had been hard, but the surprise of his visit and the thrill of knowing he wanted her to be his girlfriend had outweighed her feelings of sadness about him leaving.

But she had been waiting all week to see him again, and the day had gone by so fast. The tears she felt beginning to form on the drive home spilled over when they stepped out of the car and he walked her to the front steps.

He held her close and didn't say anything. She didn't know if she could go through this every week but also knew she had little choice. All week she had been thinking it was good they had some distance between them to keep them from moving too fast and forcing them to get to know each other through letters and the limited amount of time they had together, but right now she didn't care about any of that. She wanted to be with him. Period.

"I'm coming to your match on Thursday," he reminded her. "And you should have a letter waiting for you on Monday."

Amber looked into his eyes, feeling amazed by his thoughtfulness. He had known how she would be feeling right now. "Thank you," she said.

He kissed her gently. "I had a great time today, Amber."

"Me too," she said, managing a smile and enjoying one last kiss. He lingered a bit longer than normal. And it was just enough to help her feel more secure about letting him out of her sight for five days.

In the morning she went to church and was pleased to see Stacey and Kenny there. With the two of them, they had ten high-schoolers in Sunday school class, and eight of them were upperclassmen. Some weeks they only had four or five total, so she was excited.

"My mom and dad said they might come for the service at ten-thirty," Stacey said with hope in her voice. "They didn't promise anything, but they didn't say no, so that's something at least."

Amber gave her a hug and told her she was proud of her for inviting them. "And even if they don't come, I'm glad you're here."

"Thanks, I am too," Stacey said. "I'm surprised there aren't more here though."

"A lot of people go to bigger churches in town."

"I like it," Stacey said. "I think my dad will too. He doesn't like crowds much."

At ten-thirty Amber spotted Stacey's dad as he stepped into the church foyer. She nudged Stacey who had her back to the door at the moment. Stacey turned around and saw him coming their way.

"Where's Mom?" Stacey asked.

"She said 'maybe next time'."

Stacey gave him a hug, and they went into the main room where services were held. Amber went to sit by her own parents and Ben, who would be leaving for college in another week. Ben shared about his summer at camp as part of the service, and Amber was very touched and encouraged by what he had to say. She'd heard him say most of it already, but hearing him talk in front of so many people about his passion for knowing Jesus better and letting Him lead the way, rather than 'coasting on a wave of religion', like he felt he'd been doing the last few years, made Amber see how sincere his deepened faith was.

Amber knew Ben's words had been a powerful testimony of God's work in his life, but she didn't realize just how powerful until the end of the service when Kenny walked to the front of the church during the final song. He talked to the pastor briefly, and then Pastor Cooke motioned for Ben to come up and talk to him. Ben did and they were still talking after the service ended.

Amber found out later, some from Ben and some from Stacey, that Kenny felt like he had done the same thing as Ben--given his heart to Jesus as a child, but then sports and other ambitions had crowded God out, and he'd been making up his own rules and chasing his own dreams instead of letting God have any say in it.

Kenny made a recommitment to God through an emotional prayer, and then afterwards he and Ben went to get lunch together and talked more. Kenny told Ben he wanted to have a really good relationship with Stacey--continuing with the changes they had already made and also putting God at the center of it from now on.

"He said you and Seth had a huge impact on him," Ben told her that afternoon. "He saw you together on your birthday and all day yesterday, and he was so impressed by the maturity of your relationship that he talked to Stacey about it last night and found out how much you both look to God in your life, and he knew that had to be the reason."

Amber was amazed by her brother's words and shared that with Seth in a long letter she wrote to him late that afternoon down by the creek. She had only written to Seth by regular mail twice before, and both of those had been somewhat short. But this one matched the ones he usually sent her, and she didn't hold back, speaking purely from her heart about their time together yesterday and the absolute joy she felt in having a relationship with him. She knew he was very special and wanted to be sure he knew how she felt.

Sitting there by the water in "her spot" that she had spent many hours in the past thinking and dreaming about the future, she tried to figure out what God was doing. Why now? After having no guys show any interest in her for the last two years of high school, why did she suddenly have a serious relationship one week into her junior year?

Why this way? Why Seth? Why not someone she went to school or church with? And what made Seth want to be with her, and what made her want to be with him? Was it simply because he was the only guy to make the effort, or was it more than that? She finished her letter with words she felt strongly in her heart.

You are very special to me, Seth. You can't know how much our time together and all your letters have meant to me. Thanks for seeing me, for seeing my heart. I believe God has brought us together to bless us, and to bless others around us. People can see Jesus in us as individuals, and I think they can see Him even more as they watch us together. Does that sound crazy?

I've imagined the guy of my dreams many, many times, but the fact is--you are much, much more than I ever imagined. And if this is just a dream, I hope I don't wake up anytime soon.

Thanking God for you, Amber

***

Amber felt apprehensive about going to school on Monday. Even though she wouldn't be seeing Christian until after lunch, she worried about it all morning, wondering if he would continue to show interest in her and if she would have to keep reminding him she was taken, or if their time together would be awkward from now on. It could be a long term if that was the case.

She had prayed about it last night and this morning and kept whispering little pleas for help throughout the day. She tried to remind herself he hadn't known she had been tempted to say yes. He may have completely forgotten about it.

Taking her stool in chemistry class that afternoon, she nervously waited for his arrival, which was usually close to when the bell rang. She opened her textbook and looked over her answers to the questions she had done at the end of the chapter as homework over the weekend. Mr. Dunn had said there could possibly be a pop-quiz today. Christian strolled in about a minute later, took his seat beside her, and gave her his friendly smile and kind greeting.

"Hey," she replied, hoping her voice sounded normal enough. "How was your weekend?"

"All right," he said. "Yours?"

"Good," she replied.

That was all the chance they had to talk. Mr. Dunn always started class on time and was very strict about tardiness. They had a short quiz Amber felt she did well on, and then Mr. Dunn gave them his planned lecture for the day, using a few up-front experiments as visual aides to help them grasp the concepts.

After class Amber collected her things, put them into her backpack, and exited the classroom. Christian followed her out, and he spoke to her once they were in the hallway.

"Amber?"

She glanced up at him, feeling determined to be more clear and straightforward with him today if he continued to show any interest in her.

"I want to apologize to you about what I said on Friday. I shouldn't have said that. I wouldn't want you cheating on your boyfriend. I just thought maybe you weren't that serious, and I could encourage you to go out with me instead."

He smiled and she did too. "I'm sorry, Christian. I think you're really nice and everything, but Seth and I are pretty serious."

"Yeah, that's the impression I got from the way you turned me down."

"I should have made that more clear to you when you asked me to the dance initially." She laughed. "But to be honest, you really surprised me."

"Why were you surprised? I'd been trying to impress you all week."

She felt shocked. She hadn't picked up on anything last week until he actually asked her to the dance. "Basically, Christian, I think I'm pretty clueless when it comes to that kind of stuff. I'm sorry if I gave you the impression I was interested."

"I think you were just being yourself, Amber. You are a very nice girl--friendly, sweet. And I'm new, so I misread all that. Don't apologize for being who you are."

"Okay," she said. "Now that all that's out of the way, I'd like to have you for a friend, Christian. If you want."

He smiled. "I'd really like that. Making new friends isn't the easiest thing to do."

"May I ask you something?" she said.

"Sure."

"Is Christian only your name, or do you happen to be one?"

"I am," he said. "Hard to tell, huh?"

"No," she said quickly. "Not at all. Have you found a church you like yet?"

"We've gone to a few. Still looking for the right one, I guess."

"Where do you live?"

"About a mile from here."

"My church would be a bit out of your way, but I can recommend a few."

"Thanks, Amber," he said, stopping in front of his next class. "I'm glad we got that other stuff cleared up and I can have you as a friend. So far, this is the best thing that's happened since I moved here."

She told Christian good-bye and kept walking toward her class, saying a quick prayer of thanks to God for working that out so well. She also prayed for Christian, that he could make more friends soon.

They had an away volleyball game on Tuesday night. Both she and Stacey had made varsity this year, but she hadn't played much during the two matches they had last week. The team was loaded with seniors, and although she had usually started on JV last year, she hadn't had a chance to prove herself to her new coach, who was not only new to her but new to Sandy High.

She was surprised when Coach Hill put her in midway through the first set on account of the starter who played her position twisting her ankle. He could have put in another senior who usually subbed-in, but he chose her instead. She was more surprised when he left her in for the remainder of the match. She played her heart out and did well, and they had their first win of the season.

Stacey had been starting since the first game, and Amber had seen a definite difference in her attitude and interaction with their teammates. Stacey tended to be very serious during a game, getting down on herself or other players if they weren't doing well, but this season she appeared to be having the time of her life. She gave out high-fives like candy between points, and got them going after a slump with encouraging words more than once.

Turning her life over to God three weeks ago had made a difference in Stacey's life that was more dramatic than Amber anticipated, but having Kenny do the same thing on Sunday made the changes even more profound. Amber didn't know if Stacey's parents were going to get back together like she hoped, but her own love-life was well in order. And Amber couldn't be happier for her.

It was late by the time she got home, but Amber took the time to check her email and read the brief one from Seth. She hadn't mailed her handwritten letter to him until this morning, so she knew he wouldn't get it until at least tomorrow.

She went upstairs and found a letter from Seth waiting for her on her pillow. She decided to get into her pajamas and finish up her math assignment before reading it. His emails tended to be informative--what he'd done that day and little reminders of his affection for her. But in his letters he poured his heart out, and she cherished each one.

After she crawled into bed, she took the letter out of the envelope and fully expected to enjoy Seth's words he had probably written after their time together on Saturday. He confirmed that in the first sentence.

Dear Amber,

It's Sunday night, and it's been exactly twenty-four hours since I've seen you. So why do I still feel your lips on mine? Why can I still smell that perfume you had on at the theater? Why do my fingers still feel your soft skin?

I walked around in a daze today. I don't remember much of what happened. I kept reliving yesterday over and over in my mind and my heart. I'm wondering if you did the same.

When I used to imagine what having a girlfriend would be like, I never imagined this. I thought about what we would do and where we would go, not what my heart would feel. I never imagined doing something embarrassing in front of her like trying to water-ski, and yet not worrying she'd think I was totally lame, because I knew she wouldn't. I never imagined being in an uncomfortable situation where her friend's parents were fighting, and yet having her sweet and calm presence in the midst of that make me feel at ease. I never imagined a relationship that feels so good and brings me such joy.

Is it just me, Amber, or are you feeling mesmerized by all of this too? Is a relationship as sweet as this God's way of bringing a little bit of Heaven to Earth? Is this a taste of Paradise? Somehow I can't imagine anything coming closer.

I read some awesome verses this morning I want to share with you. They are from Ephesians One in The Message:

"He (God)...takes us to the high places of blessing in him. Long before he laid the earth's foundations, he had us in mind...Long, long ago he decided to adopt us into his family through Jesus Christ...He wanted us to enter into the celebration of his lavish gift-giving by the hand of his beloved Son."

When I read that, I thought of us--you and me together. You are a blessing to me, Amber. Our friendship is a blessing. You are a lavish gift from God to me, and I hope I am the same to you. Let's run with this! I want to let God take us to the high places--now, and for many years to come if that's what He has planned. There are no limits to what God can do in us, for us, and through us! We'll hang on to Him and each other and everything will be all right. He promises that.

Loving you,
Seth

Chapter Eleven

Seth was the first thought Amber had on Wednesday morning, and he remained there most of the day. She had read his letter twice last night and reread it before leaving for school. She felt better about the letter she had written to him. *No, Seth. You are not the only one,* she thought, refolding the letter and tucking it inside her backpack.

She read it twice more by lunchtime, and one particular phrase stood out to her every time: *Let God take us to the high places.* She agreed with Seth she had never imagined God blessing her in such a special, joy-filled way. And Seth didn't know about how their relationship had affected Kenny yet. Even having the chance to spend more time with one of her childhood friends had been a result of her relationship with Seth. God was already taking them to the high places, and she couldn't imagine it getting any better. But as Seth said, there were no limits with God.

Meeting Colleen for lunch, Amber debated about sharing Seth's letter with her. She hadn't let anyone read any of what Seth had written, except for the poem she had showed to Ben. Some of the letter seemed too personal for her to share with Colleen, but the parts about God seemed too good to keep to herself. She ended up reading that section out loud rather than having Colleen read the entire letter for herself.

"Wow," Colleen stated, letting the word hang in the air for a moment. "May I make one request?"

"What?"

"Let me pick out my own bridesmaid's dress? I don't know why this is, but women who are getting married suddenly seem to lose all fashion sense."

Amber shoved her playfully. "Oh, stop. He's not asking me to marry him! He's just--"

"Making it very clear he doesn't want this ending anytime soon."

"Yeah."

"Like for 50 years!"

Amber laughed, not admitting those same thoughts had crossed her mind. But she knew this letter wasn't about their future together. It was about now.

"When my parents used to talk about how they started dating when they were seventeen, that always seemed bizarre to me. Suddenly it doesn't seem so strange."

Colleen crumpled up her Doritos bag and tossed it into her brown lunch sack. "In all seriousness, Amber, I think that is very cool." Taking the letter from her hands before she could stop her, Colleen scanned the words and found the part she was looking for.

"I say run with it!"

Amber appreciated her support but really wanted to reach out and snatch the letter back. Colleen smiled and let her eyes fall back on the paper in her hands. She had already seen it. Too late.

"What's this about his lips on yours?" she teased. "Your soft skin?" Peeking over the top of the letter, Colleen raised her eyebrows. "Is there anything you're not telling me?"

Amber grabbed the letter and refolded it, tucking it securely into her backpack once again. Glancing up and smiling shyly at her friend, she said, "It's very innocent, I promise. Don't forget, he's a poet."

"I guess so! Can you pass me some of that magic fairy dust? I want a boyfriend too!"

Amber laughed. "He's out there, Colleen. Just wait for God to bring him along at the right time."

"Yeah, like when I'm thirty."

Knowing Colleen hadn't had her first date yet--and she was turning seventeen next month, Amber gave her a hug and said, "I never thought it would happen to me either. But you never know. You could spill your Dr. Pepper on some guy this weekend and boom--he's under your spell."

They both laughed hysterically.

"Oh, Amber. Only you could get away with that. That is so you, it's not even funny!"

They kept laughing all the way back to their locker, and Amber remained in a good mood the rest of the afternoon. Even Coach Hill's tyrannical behavior after all the silly mistakes they'd made yesterday didn't get her down.

Her mood faltered slightly when she and Stacey drove home after practice. Stacey told her if they saw no sign of Joe by the end of this weekend, her dad would be going back to his apartment on Sunday night. Stacey wasn't surprised, but not totally down about it either. She had talked to Kenny last night for a long time and had come to a somewhat peaceful conclusion.

"For the last three years I've wanted them to get remarried for *me*. I haven't even been thinking about them. I'd love to see them get back together, but I was telling Kenny last night if it doesn't happen, I know I'll be okay."

"I know you will too, Stace. You're much stronger than I am."

"It's not me, Amber. I feel so different. I used to think I'd never be happy unless everything around me was perfect.

But now, it's like none of that matters. I'm happy. I really am! And all that's changed is I have God now."

Amber smiled. "So that's it, you're giving up your crusade to get your mom and dad back together?"

"I didn't say that," Stacey laughed. "But I think my motive is changing. Any efforts I spend from now on are going to be with them in mind. I want *them* to remember how much they love each other and to be happy again for themselves, not for me."

"That's a very mature attitude, Stace. What is happening to us? It's like we're growing up or something!"

"I know. Scary, isn't it?"

***

On Thursday Amber felt like a nervous wreck all day. They had a match tonight, and it was against the top-ranked team in their league. After her performance on Tuesday and hard work at practice the previous afternoon, Coach Hill had informed her she would be on the starting lineup tonight. She knew they were going to get creamed, and many of her friends would be there along with her parents and Ben, not to mention Seth. She thought having him be there might not be a great idea after all. Even though she had been playing volleyball since sixth grade, she usually got nervous before a match, and knowing Seth would be there tonight made it worse.

She felt better once he arrived. His loving embrace helped her to relax and so did his words. She had emailed him last night, warning him not to be expecting a very exciting match. The opposing team hadn't only placed first in their league the last several seasons; they'd also won the last two State Championships.

"Look at it this way," he said. "The sooner you let them win, the more time we can have together afterwards."

She knew Coach Hill wouldn't appreciate that kind of attitude--he had this crazy notion they could win at least one game against this team, but Seth's words did help her to relax and remember this was supposed to be fun.

Walking onto the court twenty minutes later, Amber and her teammates received cheers from the home-team fans. As they went through their warm-up exercises, she tried to remember what Seth had said in his letter about not needing to worry about her thinking any differently about him because he couldn't water-ski, and that was true. She didn't care if he could water-ski or not, and she knew he wouldn't like her any more or any less depending on how she did tonight.

But the butterflies remained, especially when the time came to take the court and Coach Hill informed her she would be the first to serve--a high honor she felt totally unworthy of. She had served well on Tuesday, but her coach had obviously not seen her crack under pressure, as she had often done in the past.

"You can do this, Ambs," Stacey encouraged her following the team huddle break. "Knock 'em dead, baby!"

Amber smiled at Stacey's attempt to make her laugh and squeezed her friend's hand. Earlier during the JV match while they were waiting outside for Seth to arrive, Stacey had told her that her mom and dad's plans had changed since yesterday. Her dad would be going home tonight instead of remaining at the house through the weekend. She admired Stacey's courage. With the look on her face right now, no one would guess how much her heart was breaking.

Thinking about Stacey's courage, Amber recalled the many times she and Stacey had played on the court as teammates. They were skilled in different ways in each of the sports they played. In softball, Stacey was good at catching and throwing a long distance, while she was good at pitching and hitting. In basketball, Stacey was best at ball-handling and shooting, but she was most comfortable on defense: rebounding and making steals. And in volleyball, Stacey could block well and set a ball perfectly every time, while she was best at serving and diving for balls spiked over the net by the other team.

But Stacey often outplayed her for one reason. Stacey played fearlessly--all the time. Amber had watched her friend shine in the most crucial moments of a game--volleyball or any other, while she herself choked in those same nail-biting moments. Stacey had often pulled her through the last few innings of a close softball game. Amber would look into the eyes of her confident friend crouched behind home-plate and manage to throw her best pitches--almost as if they were in Stacey's backyard instead of in the heat of a tough game.

Amber stepped away from Stacey to take her position, suddenly feeling very much at ease. Stacey would not falter in this moment. She would rise to the occasion. And compared to what Stacey was going through with her parents, playing in a tough volleyball game was nothing. If her friend could allow God to carry her through that, she could do the same now.

The words from Seth's letter came to mind once again. *Let God take us to the high places.*

She smiled. *Yes, Jesus. Take me there!*

Glancing up at Seth then, she saw him talking to her dad. She watched him for a moment and smiled. If God could bring someone wonderful into her life, then He certainly could give her courage and strength to play her best.

The game got underway, and Amber served and played defense during the first game better than she'd ever played in her life. Their opponent seemed to be caught off-guard, first by her opening serves and then by her ability to dig for balls they weren't anticipating being returned. Her efforts fired up her teammates also, and before they knew what was happening, they found themselves leading by ten points.

The other team slowly got it together and shortened the gap, but with the score of the first game at 23-21, Amber's turn to serve came again. "You can do this, no problem," Stacey said, coming back to give her a high-five.

Amber slapped her hand and was surprised when Stacey grabbed her fingers and held on to them in midair. "You're my hero, Amber. We've got 'em!"

She smiled and felt fearless once again. Her two aces to end the game proved it. She was mobbed by her teammates with Stacey leading the way. They had done the impossible-- winning a game against the top-rated team. Classmates and parents were on their feet, going absolutely crazy. And in the middle of it all, she and Stacey were clinging to each other and crying.

"I love you, Stace," she said in her friend's ear. "You're going to be all right."

"I know, Amber," she said. "God is making it all right."

They both started the second game and were doing well once again until Amber injured herself. She dove for a ball and slipped, making her fall the wrong way and sprain her wrist. She tried to shake it off and tell Coach Hill she was all right, she really wanted to keep playing, but he wasn't buying it.

"Come on out, Wilson. You need a break anyway."

She took a seat on one of the chairs set up on the sidelines, bending and flexing her wrist to keep it loose. One of the seniors on the team she hadn't made a solid connection with yet handed her a water-bottle.

"Great job out there, Amber. Those were some wicked serves."

"Thanks," she said.

She really wanted to get back in there, but she did need the rest. Her teammates kept it close for awhile, but then began to fall apart. Once it became clear they would likely not make up the hole they'd gotten themselves into, Coach Hill gave some of the others a rest, and Stacey came to sit beside her.

"They're killing us now, but it was fun while it lasted."

"We'll get back into it next game," she said. "They're pretty weak at serving."

Stacey laughed. "They're not weak, Ambs. You're just awesome. What got into you, anyway?"

She smiled. "Just a little bit of Jesus."

"Well whatever He's doing, tell Him not to stop."

They both started the third game and although her wrist still twinged on each play, Amber did not give in, and they kept it close the whole way. The other team won, but only by two points. Her wrist was throbbing at that point, and although she didn't let on her pain to anyone, least of all her coach, he took her out for the fourth game anyway.

"We've got other matches this season, Wilson," he said. "Let's keep you healthy."

Chapter Twelve

The assistant coach took a look at her wrist during the fourth game and gave her an ice-pack for the swelling. Fortunately it was her right one, not her left, so her serve wouldn't be affected if this didn't feel better by next week, but she was sure it would. It hurt, but not bad enough to be broken. She knew what that felt like.

The fourth game didn't take too long. Her non-injured teammates were out of energy, but she knew they should be proud of how well they'd played against this tough team. If they could beat them in one game and come close to winning another, they could certainly take some of the other teams in this league in the coming weeks.

Seth came down to meet her afterwards. Her family already had and said they would see her at home. Seth asked the same question her mom had, pointing to the ice-pack over her wrist.

"Are you going to be all right?"

"Yeah, it's fine," she said, removing the cold pack and laying it on the chair she'd been sitting on.

He took her wrist in his hand and kissed it gently. She knew she was very sweaty, and her hair had to be atrocious, but he didn't seem to mind.

"Thanks for coming," she said. "I don't think I could describe this very well in an email."

"You were amazing," he said, letting go of her wrist and giving her a hug. "Do you have a twin?"

"What?" she laughed.

"I don't believe the girl I saw play tonight or water-ski on Saturday can be the same girl who spilled her Pepsi on me and tripped over a rock in the woods."

"And during a skit," she reminded him.

"Yeah, I'm not sure I'm buying that whole damsel-in-distress routine anymore."

She smiled. "Too late. I got you anyway."

He shook his head and kissed her on the forehead. "You have no idea, Amber."

She left him to go take a quick shower and change. Stacey waited for her, and they left the locker room together, finding "their boys" just outside the gymnasium waiting for them. Seth and Kenny seemed to be getting to know each other, and Amber knew it would be a good thing for them to become friends, especially for Kenny who needed other Christian guys to encourage him in his renewed faith. Amber gave Stacey one last hug without saying anything once they stepped outside, and they separated from her and Kenny in the parking lot.

Walking with Seth to his car parked along the street, she felt him take her hand in the cool night air. "I have some bad news," he said.

"What?"

"I have to work this Saturday."

They hadn't made any official plans to see each other this weekend, but she'd been hoping for some time with him.

"Actually, I don't have to," he said. "But I feel like I should. Mr. Davidson has a big print-run to do this weekend, and he asked for my help if I was free. I'm supposed to get back to him by tomorrow."

"That's okay if you want to," she said, knowing she couldn't expect to be seeing him every weekend plus having him come to her games--which he'd already told her he wanted to do as much as he could. Ever since he had decided to keep the job on a part-time basis, she knew this was a possibility.

"You won't be mad?" he asked, coming to a stop beside the car. She could tell he wanted her to be completely honest.

"No," she said. She didn't want him to feel bad about it. "Sad. But not mad."

"I think I will then," he said. "The good news is I only have to work until three and I could come out for a little while on Saturday evening, or I have another idea to run by you."

"What's that?" she asked, feeling glad she might get time with him after all.

"How would you like to ride MAX into Portland on Saturday afternoon, meet my parents, spend the night at my house, and go to church with me on Sunday morning?"

She stared at him. "Are you serious?"

"My parents are anxious to meet you, and this would give us almost as much time together as if we had all day Saturday."

"You've already talked to your parents?"

"I didn't want to ask you before I asked them, but don't feel pressured if you'd rather not. It's just an idea."

Other than her apprehensiveness about meeting his parents, her first reaction was to say yes. She knew she would be facing this eventually. It may as well be now, and she definitely wanted the extra time with him. But then she remembered something.

"That's a great idea, and I'd love to, except Ben is leaving for college on Sunday afternoon. We're going out to lunch after church, and I'd like to be at home to say good-bye to him."

"Okay, that's fine," he said. "We can do that another time."

She felt bad. "I'm sorry."

"Don't be. I wouldn't expect you to miss out on that."

"Does this mean I don't get to see you on Saturday?"

He smiled, leaned close to her ear, and whispered, "Absolutely not. I'll take whatever I can get."

He kissed her then for the first time, besides when he'd arrived. And he kissed her differently than he ever had before. It was very slow and tender and lasted much longer. She kissed him back in the same way and had an indescribable feeling when he slowly ended it.

"Let's go get ice cream," he said.

She smiled and felt her lips tingling. "Okay."

They drove to Dairy Queen and sat in a booth beside the window, eating Blizzards and sharing French fries. She told him about how she felt during the match and why she knew she played so well--better than she ever had before.

"You looked fearless," he said. "I don't think the other team knew what to do with you. You should have seen the way they looked at each other each time you got up to serve."

"I've always been good at serving, but not always when it counts. It felt good to let go of all that worry and fear and pressure to--I don't know, prove myself, I guess. I was just having fun tonight!"

He laughed. "The other team wasn't."

She smiled. "I thought about that verse: *'God takes us to the high places.'* And I asked Him to take me there. He did it, Seth! He lifted me up out of my fear and said, 'Just play, Amber!' That's what felt really amazing."

104

Seth smiled but appeared to have something else on his mind. "I hope that letter wasn't too--" he searched for the right words. "Over the top? It all came pouring out of me, and I almost didn't send it. I thought it might freak you out a little."

"Did you mean it?" she asked.

"Every word."

"Then I'm glad you did. I've been thinking about it ever since."

He sighed. "I'm glad to hear you say that. I can't keep stuff like that to myself."

"I wouldn't want you to. Please don't stop, okay?"

He smiled. "I won't. I felt better after I read yours. And I agree with you one-hundred percent, Amber. This is about us and more. More than we can imagine at this point, I'm sure."

She told him about Stacey's dad going home tonight and Stacey's acceptance of it. "I'm really proud of her--and amazed by what God has done in her heart in such a short amount of time. I always thought sharing about Jesus with Stacey and making Him a part of her life would only affect her, I never imagined I would be changed too. I see God totally different than I did a month ago."

Seth reached across the table and took her hands in his. *"The one who existed from the beginning is the one we have heard and seen. We saw him with our own eyes and touched him with our own hands. He is Jesus Christ, the Word of life."*

Amber stared at him, hardly believing she had heard him speak those words. That was the verse the youth pastor had quoted on their final night of camp before he had given the invitation for anyone who wanted to know Jesus better. He had given out three-by-five cards with the verse printed on them to those who had gone forward, and Amber had posted it on the wall above her desk.

She smiled. "You memorized it?"

"Yes."

"Me too."

She repeated the words back to Seth, and he appeared to be in a state of disbelief also. He slid across the seat and stood to his feet. She did the same and took the hand he offered her on the way out. They walked to his car, but before he opened the door for her, he pulled her close to him, looked into her eyes, and spoke softly.

"I never imagined, Amber. I never imagined this. I never imagined you."

She felt tingly all over and didn't look away from his soft brown eyes. "And I never imagined you," she whispered.

He kissed her tenderly again and lingered like he had earlier. She felt overwhelmed by the intensity of the feelings she was beginning to have for him. Not just physical desire but something beyond that. Their hearts were connecting in a way she'd never experienced with anyone.

He drove her home, and knowing she would be seeing him again on Saturday helped her to say good-bye without tears this time. So did his kiss at the door.

"Is it okay for me to kiss you like that?" he asked. "Please be honest, Amber. I don't want to do anything you're not ready for."

"It's fine," she said, unable to hold back a smile. "It's *really* fine."

He smiled back. "Yeah, for me too," he said, holding her gently against him. "I'll be careful about when and where I kiss you like that."

"That would be a good idea," she said. "I may like it a little too much."

"I'll be careful, Amber," he repeated. "I promise."

She believed he would be, and she would continue to pray for that area of their relationship. Not having sex until she was married was something she was committed to. She wanted to wait for God's best for her, but she also began to realize that may not be as easy as she thought.

"You know, I was thinking," she said, "and it's fine to say no to this, but how about if you stay here on Saturday night and go to church with me on Sunday and out to lunch with my family since I can't go to Portland?"

"I thought of that," he said. "But I wouldn't want to intrude on your time with your family."

"You wouldn't be intruding," she said. "My family really likes you."

"Maybe you should check with them first, just to make sure."

"If they're okay with it, do you want to?"

He smiled. "Yes."

"I'll let you know by tomorrow then," she said. "And if you have a lot of homework this weekend, we can stay here on Saturday instead of going somewhere so you can get it done. I'm happy to just be with you."

"And I'm happy to be with you," he said, kissing her briefly one last time. "Good night, Amber."

"Good night, Seth."

He stepped away and she waited until his car was out of sight to go inside. Her parents and Ben were still up, and she went ahead and asked them about Saturday and Sunday.

"We haven't had much time with him yet," her mom said. "You've been keeping him all to yourself. I think that would be nice."

"Dad?"

"Fine with me, Jewel. Will Seth have any time to get homework done?"

She told him what she had told Seth outside and sat down beside her brother. "Is having Seth here on Sunday all right with you?" she asked Ben. "He said he didn't want to intrude."

Ben smiled. "Somehow Seth doesn't strike me as the intruding type. And I'd like to get to know him a little better myself if he's going to be seeing my sister this much."

"I think that's his plan."

Telling everyone good-night, she trudged her aching body up the stairs, changed into her pajamas, and fell into bed. She was glad she had been able to get her homework done after school, because she wouldn't have been able to do anything now.

Before she went to sleep, however, she did spend a few minutes praying, thanking God for helping her to play her best tonight and have fun in the process. She also thanked Him for her time with Seth and prayed about the time they would have together this weekend.

Those kisses he gave me were really good, God. Help us to keep them controlled and innocent. Seth makes me feel things I haven't felt before, and it scares me a little. But if you have given us those desires and the warning to save them for when we're married, then I suppose you can help us to do that.

I pray for Stacey and Kenny in this too. I'm amazed they haven't had sex with as long as they've been together and considering what Stacey told me last weekend, but I know they're just now starting to get emotionally and spiritually close too. Maybe that makes waiting harder--I don't know. But if so, I can imagine them wanting to give in to those desires more now too. Please help them to wait.

And I pray for Stacey, especially tonight and in the next couple of days as her dad is once again living somewhere else. May she know you are with her and that you are doing everything you can to help her mom and dad to know you and learn to love each other again. I ask this for Stacey and for her sister, Chelsea. And I ask it especially for Mr. and Mrs. Collins. I wish they could be happy like my mom and dad.

Thank you, thank you, thank you for this day, Jesus! For the game and my time with Seth. You have been taking me to the high places for a long time--even before I realized you were doing it. Keep taking me higher, to what you have planned for me. Keep drawing me closer to you.

Chapter Thirteen

Amber and Christian worked diligently on their chemistry experiment and finished before the class time ended on Friday afternoon. It had been a two-day process that made Amber thankful to have a lab partner like Christian. He loved stuff like this and always seemed to know what he was doing, but he didn't take over and do it all. He explained things as they went along, and the experiment did help her to understand what they had been studying this week--much better than listening to Mr. Dunn and from reading the book.

"Do you have any idea what you'd like to do after high school?" she asked, wondering if he had a particular interest in science.

"No clue," he said. "How about you?"

"No clue for me too," she said, happy to hear she wasn't the only one. Colleen wanted to go to medical school. Stacey didn't know for sure but thought she might like to do something with animals--a vet, a horse breeder and trainer, and a wildlife biologist were among her current ambitions.

When Amber said 'no clue,' she meant no clue. A teacher? Maybe. A rocket scientist--definitely not. She hoped she would figure it out at some point before she finished college--if she even went to college. She didn't know if she wanted to or not.

"Are you seeing Seth this weekend?" Christian asked her. He sounded genuinely interested, and she told him about their plans.

"How long have you been dating?"

She didn't know if she wanted to share the exact timeframe with him. It had been a month since their canoe-ride on the lake at camp, and she considered that to be their first date in a way. But she didn't want to give Christian the impression they might not be as serious as they were simply because they hadn't been together very long.

"I met him this summer," she said. "And we've been dating ever since. But it seems like a lot longer."

"Yeah, I know what you mean," he said.

"Did you have a girlfriend in Alaska?"

"Yes, but we hadn't been dating that long before I found out we were moving, so I decided to end it rather than bring on a more difficult decision later about having a long-distance relationship."

"Do you miss her?"

"Not as much now that we're here, but those last couple months of still seeing her at school and church were tough, especially when she started going out with another guy."

"Are you a junior or a senior?" she asked, realizing she didn't know.

"A senior."

"Well, maybe you'll meet someone here," she said. "I'd go out with you--if I didn't already have a boyfriend."

"Yeah, I asked a girl out last weekend, and she used the same excuse."

Amber laughed. "Well, I know lots of great girls who aren't taken, including my best friend."

"Oh?" he said.

"Yeah, Colleen Garcia. Have you met her?"

"Doesn't sound familiar," he said. "What's she look like?"

"Absolutely beautiful," she said. "Long dark hair, dark eyes, beautiful tan skin. Her family went to Mexico this summer to visit her grandparents. Her dad is a teacher here. Mr. Garcia? He teaches math."

"I have Mr. Garcia for Calculus," he said. "I think maybe I did see his daughter one day this week when she came in after class."

"Very possible," she said. "You two would have a lot in common. She's a science and math genius too."

"And she's a Christian?"

"Yes. In fact, she goes to one of the churches I told you to have your family try. Good Shepherd? It's on the highway on the way to Gresham."

He smiled. "Maybe I'll talk my parents into going there," he said.

The bell rang and they left the classroom together. Amber felt the need to say one last thing on the subject of her best friend. "If you do end up meeting her at some point and decide to ask her out, don't tell her I said anything, okay? I don't want her to think you're only interested because I told you to ask her out."

"Okay. I won't."

"And, if you do take her out sometime, you better treat her right, or you'll have me to deal with."

"And Mr. Garcia," he added. "I don't think I'd want to get on his bad side."

She laughed. "Definitely not."

"Did you tell her what I said to you last Friday?" he asked, appearing embarrassed.

"No. I don't think I've mentioned you except saying I have a great lab partner in Chemistry."

Amber finished the day with a light heart. After volleyball practice where her coach and teammates had lots of nice words for her concerning her performance last night, she and Stacey headed for the hills as usual, feeling glad the week was over.

Since Seth wasn't coming until later tomorrow, and she and Stacey were planning to go to the football game together tonight, Stacey asked if she wanted to spend the night at her house--something Amber hadn't done for quite awhile.

She said she would have to check with her mom and dad first but thought they'd say it was fine. After dinner when Stacey picked her up again, she took her sleeping bag and a change of clothes with her, telling her parents she would be home by noon on Saturday. Amber enjoyed going to the away-game with Stacey, something they hadn't done together since early on in their freshman year when they were still close friends from junior high and hadn't made a bunch of new ones in high school yet. Since then they'd been hanging around in different crowds--even before Stacey started dating Kenny last year. But Amber knew things were much different between them now. They might not do everything together, but any time they had would be a deeper kind of friendship.

Their team played well, and she and Stacey did a lot of cheering for Kenny, the quarterback of their high school team. Stacey went out to meet him on the field following a convincing victory, and Amber waited on the outer track for her to return. While she was standing there, she saw two people she knew walking by, and she said hello. Nicole and Spencer had been dating since last spring. She didn't have any classes with Nicole this term and had only seen her in the hallways since school started.

Nicole had P.E. at the end of the day, and they often passed each other without comment as Amber walked toward the locker room for volleyball practice. Nicole hadn't been at her birthday party, even though she'd invited her, and she hadn't been to church since Amber had returned from camp, which she thought was strange, but she hadn't said anything about it.

"Hey, Amber," Spencer said, seeming his usual self. "How's it going?"

"Good," she said.

"I saw you play last night. You were great."

"Thanks."

That was the extent of their conversation, and she said good-bye to both of them.

"See you Sunday," Spencer said, turning away with his arm around Nicole's shoulder.

"You ready?" Stacey asked, bounding beside her and startling her slightly.

"Yeah," she said. "Is Kenny coming by later?"

"No. He's tired and knows you're coming over. It's just you and me, baby!"

Amber laughed at Stacey's chipperness. She had always been nice and the kind of person anyone would be happy to have as a friend, but giddy and chipper were not words she would use to describe her--unless she had something really good to smile about. She recalled Stacey being this way every time she had seen her today.

"What is with you?" she asked. "Still on a high from the match last night? I was the star, not you. Why are you so giddy?"

Stacey laughed. "Am I?"

"Yes. You are."

Stacey smiled shyly. "I guess I'm in a bit of a good mood," she admitted.

Now Amber knew there was something going on. "Oh yeah? Care to share it with one of your oldest friends."

Stacey let out a content sigh. "Last night when Kenny took me home, we talked for a long time. I was upset about my dad leaving, and he knew that, but he said all the right things."

"Like what?"

Stacey smiled. "He said he loves me."

"Was that the first time?"

She nodded.

"And he just told you again on the field, didn't he?"

She smiled.

"That's awesome, Stace! You two are in my prayers, you know."

Stacey wiped her moist eyes. "I know, Amber. Keep us there. Ever since my parents split up, I've had this awful fear of getting married someday only to end up like them. But now, for the first time since we started dating, I feel like me and Kenny could really have a chance to be happy together for a long time, you know? I want to do this right."

"I know exactly what you mean," she said. "And you know I'm always here if you need to talk--about anything?"

"Yes," she replied and surprised her by initiating a hug. "I thank God for you, Amber. You're not just my oldest friend, you're also the best one I've ever had. And I love you."

Stacey's words brought tears to her eyes.

"I love you too, Stace," she whispered.

Chapter Fourteen

Amber and Stacey stayed up late, talking and watching movies like they often had when they were younger. Stacey shared more about her and Kenny's relationship since camp, and it was all good. Amber also told her a little more about her time with Seth and the letters he'd written her.

In the morning they slept until Stacey's younger sister came into the living room to watch cartoons. Chelsea was eleven, and she and Stacey were pretty close despite their age difference. Stacey had taken Chelsea under her wing in many ways since their parents had split up.

"Where's Mom?" Stacey asked, sitting up in her sleeping bag and leaning against the couch.

"In the garden," Chelsea answered. "She's picking all those green tomatoes and the last of the zucchini."

"I heard it might rain today," Stacey said. "Looks pretty nice now though. Maybe we can go to the lake after all."

Amber sat up and confirmed Stacey's words. She'd heard about the rain prediction too but hoped it would hold off until tonight. She wanted to take Seth down to the creek if he got out here with enough time to spare before dinner. He had told her to expect him around four-thirty.

They had cereal for breakfast and hung out for the remainder of the morning. Stacey's mom brought in a box full of tomatoes and other garden vegetables. Amber had seen her own mother doing the same all week. They still had zucchini on the counter after her mom had made everything under the sun with it. And their pantry had green tomatoes lining the floor. In a few weeks the house would smell like homemade tomato sauce after her mother got through making their year-long supply.

Amber and Stacey were sitting on the back patio listening to music and painting their nails when Stacey's dad unexpectedly appeared through the sliding glass door.

"Where's your mom?" he asked in a clipped voice.

"Inside somewhere," Stacey said. "Why?"

He didn't respond and disappeared into the house. Stacey glanced at her and was on her feet in a flash, following her dad inside and holding her wet nails in the air.

Amber didn't know what to do. If Mr. Collins hadn't arrived with such a concerned look on his face, she would have remained outside and waited for Stacey to return. But something was going on, and if it was bad news, she thought Stacey might need her support, and she was curious too, so she went inside after her.

Seeing Stacey going down the hallway, Amber followed. Stacey stopped outside her mom's bedroom door and didn't go inside. Amber caught up with her. She couldn't see into the room from where she had stopped, but she could hear her dad speak.

"Are you all right, Candi?"

"Yes," she heard Stacey's mom say. "What are you doing here?"

"You called me. And then you hung up. I tried calling you back, and then it was busy. I thought--"

"You thought what? That Joe came here and was holding us all hostage? Michael! Give up this obsession! He got mad and pushed me around a couple times. He's not going to be headline news tomorrow!"

Amber didn't move. Neither did Stacey. Chelsea came up from behind. "Is Dad--?"

Stacey turned and stopped her from going into the room, silencing her with a finger on her lips.

Amber heard Stacey's dad speak again.

"Why did you call?"

"I don't know. Just to talk, I guess. Stacey came into the room right after I dialed your number, and I didn't want her to know, so I hung up. Then she needed to use the phone and she talked to Kenny for about ten minutes."

Amber heard Stacey's dad sigh, and then things got quiet for about ten seconds. Stacey had just leaned forward to peer around the door frame when her mom blurted out, "Michael! What are you doing?"

"Kissing you."

Amber felt her eyes widen.

"Leave, Mike. Now. I mean it."

"You were kissing me back, Candice."

Another long period of silence followed. Stacey remained in place. Chelsea was about to wiggle out of her skin. Amber reached out and pulled her close and whispered in her ear. "Let this be about them, Chelse."

"I love you, Candi," her dad spoke again. "Please, can't we try? I'm not talking about moving back in yet. I just want some time with you. Me not wanting to leave after the first week didn't have anything to do with Joe. I wanted an excuse to be here."

"And you came today because--?"

"Because I was seriously worried something might be wrong. I know we didn't have a perfect marriage, Candi, but I never hurt you, and I can't stand the thought of anyone doing that."

Stacey glanced at her with tears on her cheeks. Amber put her arms around her from behind and held her close along with Chelsea on her other side. They all waited for someone to speak.

"Do you still love me, Candi? Even a little?"

More silence was followed by a whisper Amber could barely hear.

"Yes."

"Will you have dinner with me tonight?"

Amber let her own tears fall at the tenderness of his voice. He sounded like a sixteen-year-old asking a girl to the prom.

Say yes, Mrs. Collins. Say yes!

Her response was close enough.

"Okay."

Stacey turned around and hugged her and then Chelsea. Amber thought she and Chelsea might go in now, but Stacey directed them down the hall and onto the patio.

"Let them come tell us," she said, calmly taking a seat on the chair. Amber didn't know if she could stand to wait, and fortunately she didn't have to.

"Where did you three disappear to?" Mr. Collins asked, coming to find them thirty seconds later. Stacey's mom was beside him and they were holding hands. "Afraid you'd get caught eavesdropping?"

Stacey made no apologies. Standing up, she went to her parents and gave them each a long hug. Chelsea joined them, and Amber witnessed the reunion of a family.

"We're not promising anything," her dad said. "But we're going to try and make this work."

"Well, for your sake," Stacey said, "I hope it does."

***

Amber got home a little later than she planned and went upstairs to get some homework done--after telling her mom and dad the good news. She attacked her math and moved on to chemistry at two o'clock. Preferring to read, answer the questions to be prepared for the "pop-quiz", and listening to music at the same time, she selected an album on her new iPod she'd gotten from her mom and dad for her birthday. Plugging her way through the questions, she only had one more to go when she felt gentle hands on her shoulders. Turning around, she saw Seth looking down at her with a smile on his face.

She stood up without thinking and almost knocked her iPod along with a can of Pepsi to the floor. Seth caught them for her and removed the earbuds from her ears.

"There's the girl I know," he teased.

"You're early!"

"I am. The job didn't take as long as Mr. Davidson thought."

"I'm glad," she said, checking her window and seeing the blue sky peeking through the fir trees. "I want to take a walk down to the creek with you. We might not have a chance if we start getting rain anytime soon."

They left the room, and she found her mom and dad in the kitchen--kissing. She glanced at Seth. He lifted his eyebrows, and she burst out laughing.

"We have company," she said to her unembarrassed parents. "Do we need to stay here and chaperone?"

They did not step away from each other.

"Oh, no, Jewel. You go ahead. I'll keep my eye on your mother."

She rolled her eyes and grabbed Seth's hand. "Come on, sweet thing. Not for your innocent eyes."

They headed for the door. Her dad peered around the corner and reminded her about part of the trail that had partially slid away sometime in the last two weeks. She had discovered it last Sunday when she hiked the trail by herself in the afternoon. "Be careful, Jewel. Don't make Seth carry you out of there."

"I won't," she said, giving him a teasing smile. "But I might make him carry me down."

"Jewel," her dad warned. "Safety first."

"I'm teasing," she said. "If we're not back in an hour, send the rescue squad."

She led Seth to the beginning of the trail that switched itself back and forth down to the creek bed. Before they began their descent, he pulled her close to him and said, "Do I get a kiss today?"

She smiled. "If you want one."

He didn't answer that with words, and she enjoyed the feeling of his tender lips. He kept his affection brief but satisfying.

"I missed you," he said.

"I missed you."

"Do your parents always kiss like that in the middle of the kitchen?"

"You have no idea," she said. "They act like they're still in high school."

"Is that when they met?"

She smiled. "Yes."

He kissed her again. "I hope I don't wake up anytime soon either, Amber."

She wondered if he read her most recent letter as much as she read his. Turning around, she led the way to her favorite spot on the planet. On the way down the wooded path, she told him about Stacey's mom and dad and was careful to remain on the part of the trail that hadn't slid down the hillside. Seth stopped her when she had finished her brief summary of what had taken place this morning.

"You know you're a part of that," he said. "Faithfully being her friend all these years, sharing about Jesus with her so she could be changed. And now, that's spilling onto her mom and dad."

"I'm amazed by what God has done with my pathetic efforts," she said, feeling unworthy of his praise. "A month ago I was so mad at her halfway through the week of camp, and then three days later she knew Jesus. And it's been nothing but blue skies since, but that has been more because of her faith, not mine."

He smiled and kissed her sweetly. "Well, I've been having a rather sunny month, and that has everything to do with you."

She hugged him and enjoyed the feeling of his return embrace. His kisses were wonderful and gave her new feelings she wasn't sure what to do with, but his gentle hugs made her feel secure and safe and special to him.

"It's been nothing but blue skies for me too, Seth," she said, and silently thought: *I hope it doesn't rain anytime soon.*

They continued on their way. When they reached the creek, she took him down to where the trail ended: at the base of a private cascading waterfall.

"Is this all your property?" he asked.

"Not down here," she said. "This is National Forest land. Ours ends at the top of the trail."

"But you're the only ones who come down here."

"Mostly," she said. "My own little piece of heaven right in my backyard. This has always been my special place to come and think and dream."

"What do you think and dream about?"

She thought for a moment. As a child she'd thought about going on great adventures and having her friends over for a swimming party in the pool beneath the waterfall. In recent years, she'd often thought about being here with a boy and dreaming about her future.

"Mostly about what's going on in my life and wondering what the future holds," she replied. "Do you know what you want to do after high school?" she asked, suddenly realizing she'd never asked him that.

"Not really," he said, stepping behind her and wrapping his arms around her waist so they were both facing the waterfall. "Do you?"

"Not a clue," she said.

"That's all right. God will show us at the right time."

Amber closed her eyes and enjoyed the sound of the waterfall, the mild breeze tickling her cheeks, and being held in Seth's arms. It had never been this good in her dreams.

"Did you read your verse for today?" he asked.

After discovering they had both memorized the first verse in First John, Seth had emailed her yesterday with the idea of reading through the book together, one verse at a time, and sharing what they got out of it with each other.

"Yes, did you?"

"Yes. I feel like we're seeing Him, don't you? In ways we haven't before?"

She spoke the words she remembered writing in her journal. "I think He's putting His love into our hearts--love for each other and for those around us."

She turned in his arms and wanted him to kiss her again like he'd done at the top of the trail, but she knew he wouldn't. This was too secluded of a place.

"I see Him in you, Seth," she said. "Like the blazing sun."

He kissed her forehead. "Keep praying for blue skies, okay? It's been a little cloudy in the past, and I don't want to go back there."

"Okay. I'll do that. Keep praying for me too. Some days I don't feel like I do so well."

"How we feel and what others see are two different things, sweetheart. Since I've met you and felt so attracted to you, I've been watching other girls, trying to figure out what exactly I like about you--what makes you different."

"You've been watching other girls?" she teased him.

"Observing," he corrected. "Not what they look like, but what they're like--on the inside."

"And?" she asked.

"I have it partially figured out. You're genuine."

"Genuine?"

"Honest and real. Honest with God, real with those around you. You don't try to be someone you're not, and you don't expect others to be anyone but themselves. And your love for Jesus is so clear. You don't just say it, you live it."

She felt tears stinging her eyes. Up until Seth had written her that poem at camp, she'd never thought about a guy being attracted to her because of her relationship with God, and yet she couldn't imagine wanting anything more.

"From where I'm standing, Amber, you're shining His light just fine, and it's nothing but blue skies."

She smiled but felt unworthy of such praise. "I usually do okay for awhile after being at camp, but in the past those clouds have rolled back in. Why is that?"

"Maybe we forget what we really want."

She knew that was probably true. She got busy, lazy, lost her focus. "I don't want to forget this time, Seth. Don't let me, okay?"

"I don't want to forget either," he said. "Maybe that's why He brought us together. Two seeking hearts are stronger than one."

She smiled. "That sounds like the beginning of a poem."

"Yes, it does. Maybe I'll write the rest later."

"I like that we're both seeking God. I think that's what makes this so easy. We're both right before Him, so there's not a lot of clouds to get in the way of us having a great relationship."

"I think you're right about that," he said. "And I don't know about you, but I don't want any of this to be ending anytime soon."

"Me neither. I really like you, Seth. I like being with you, and I like the way you make me feel."

"How do I make you feel?"

She waited for the right word to come to her. "Special. Like I matter to you."

"That's good, because that's the way I see you, Amber. You're like a treasure I could spend years looking for and never find. But I did, and now I never want to let go."

Chapter Fifteen

Amber had a fun and perfect evening with Seth. After having dinner with her family, they drove to the lake and went for a long walk together.

"How's your wrist feeling?" he asked, lifting up the hand he held.

"Fine," she said. "It's a little sore, but it should be all right by Monday."

He stepped around to the other side and took her other hand, the one with the silver bracelet just above it that he'd given her two weeks ago. "I'll hold this one instead," he said.

She smiled at him, her heart still warm from the talk they'd had down by the creek this afternoon. Last weekend she remembered thinking seeing him on Saturdays would be fun and give them time to get to know each other. She had imagined spending similar days with him, going out with Stacey and Kenny, and becoming friends along the way.

But that letter he'd sent this week, along with the way he talked about their relationship, made her see things differently now. Yes, he would come see her on Saturdays and they would double-date with their friends. He would be at some of her volleyball matches, and they would go out for ice cream afterwards. But this thing between them had quickly risen to a level beyond dating. It thrilled her. It scared her. It made her wonder what was still to come.

Stopping in a clearing and taking in a view of the lake with the mountain jetting into the sky beyond the water, Seth drew her close to his side and said something she had been thinking too.

"I feel a lot different than when we were here the last time. Don't you?"

"Yes. I remember feeling clueless about how to act or what to say, but now I know I can be myself and that's enough."

"Me too," he said. "But one thing is the same."

"What?"

Seth turned her to face him and kissed her gently. "I can't keep myself from doing that."

She started to say something, but then stopped.

"What?"

"Nothing. Never mind."

"What were you going to say?" he pressed.

She made a mental note to herself: *Never start to say something if you're not planning to go through with it.*

"I was going to ask you something."

"What?"

She smiled and looked into his warm brown eyes. "Why couldn't you wait to kiss me after saving those lips for so long?"

"Because you're the one I was saving them for."

She smiled. "How did you know that?"

"I don't know. I just did. Do you wish I would have waited?"

"No. I needed them to know you were serious."

"I think I knew that," he said. "I needed it too."

"Why?"

"I tend to be cautious about things. Taking risks isn't my usual first step."

"Why now? Why me?"

"From the moment I met you I'd been taking risks, and they had worked out fine, so I figured--why stop now?"

"What kind of risks?"

He laughed. "What risks? You want the list?"

"The list?"

He leaned his forehead against hers, gently stroking her arms as he spoke. "Going up to the counter at Taco Bell to talk to you; sitting with you at dinner the first chance I got; giving you that poem; asking your dad for permission to come see you; asking you to be my girlfriend--don't think for a second I wasn't scared to death every single time."

She took a step back and looked into his eyes. "You talked to me at Taco Bell--on purpose?"

He smiled. "Yes, I did."

She was speechless.

He pulled her back and held her close. "I know you don't see yourself as anything special, Amber, but I do. And in the same way you find my interest in you surprising, I feel the same about you welcoming every step I've taken toward you."

She'd never considered that. He had seemed comfortable and fearless every time she'd encountered him that week. She could use a lot of words to describe Seth; insecure was not one of them--at least not until now. It seemed like every time she saw him, she discovered something new about him. Things that only made her like him more and feel closer to him--which she never thought was possible until it happened.

They finished walking around the lake, talking and laughing and sharing things she never expected to be sharing with Seth this soon. He could get her to talk about everything from her worst fears to her biggest dreams and a lot of little personal things in between. She'd never had a friend like him.

That night after she went to bed, she remained awake thinking, hardly believing her boyfriend was downstairs sleeping on the couch. Her boyfriend! That in itself still seemed crazy to her. Not to mention the fact he seemed so perfect for her, her parents really liked him, and things were going on in her heart she had never expected from a relationship.

Seeing him so early the next morning reminded her of camp. Although she'd never talked to him at breakfast, she had seen him several mornings and admired him from afar. But having him across the table, dressed in his Sunday morning clothes, with his hair damp from the shower he'd taken, showed her a side of him she hadn't seen before.

"What's that look for?" he asked, drinking the last of his orange juice.

"I'm admiring the view."

He looked embarrassed. "It's just a nice shirt."

"No. It's more than that."

"I like your hair that way," he said. "This is only the second time I've seen you wear it like that."

"The second time?" she asked, feeling positive she had not worn it pulled into a clip with the back cascading freely during the time they had spent together. She had either worn it in a ponytail or completely loose.

"*'But the time I remember most was at fireside one night'*" he quoted from the poem he had written for her.

"I thought you only noticed me praising God."

"Oh, no. I noticed everything about you that night. You look nice in yellow too."

Since that wasn't the color she was currently wearing, she knew he must be referring to that night. She couldn't remember what she had worn, but she knew he did. She had noticed during the short amount of time they'd spent together he was very observant. He watched others and kept himself out of the spotlight. He listened more than he talked.

Thinking about her Sunday morning outfit, she wondered if she should have dressed up a little more. She had stopped wearing dresses regularly and currently only owned two that fit her. Her mom had gotten her a nice dress for her birthday, but it had long sleeves and would be a little warm for today, and the other one she'd had for a couple of years, but she hadn't worn it much. Today she had chosen capri pants and a simple white shirt as she often did on Sundays during the summer. She didn't feel the need to go change, but she wondered what Seth thought of her choice.

When they were finished eating, they went outside and sat on the porch, waiting for her family and discussing when they might see each other after today. She thought they might have a volleyball match at a school in Portland on Thursday and said she would look at her schedule this afternoon. He mentioned the possibility of her meeting his parents sometime soon, and she said that would be fine--whatever he wanted to set up.

Seth took something out of his Bible and handed it to her.

"What's this?" she asked, taking the folded piece of paper from him.

"I wrote something for you last night after everyone went to bed."

"Another poem?" she asked with a hopeful smile.

"I hope you like it."

She unfolded the paper. Seth sat quietly beside her as she read:

Two Seeking Hearts

Two seeking hearts are stronger than one
And it's hard to believe He's only begun
To weave our hearts together into one, don't you see?
I believe that's what He's doing between you and me

I never imagined it would be like this
So pure and right, nothing but bliss
You're invading my heart so easy and fast
And I hope and pray the blue skies will last

We'll seek Him together, not just apart
We'll share our thoughts, we'll share our hearts
We'll learn His truth and live it out
I want us to shine and maybe even shout

That His love is real and it is here
Within our hearts it becomes clear
This isn't a mistake or just random chance
He wants us to live, He wants us to dance

And so we will dance, my jewel, my treasure
Not with meaningless talk and mere fleeting pleasure
But by seeking things above: His love and His heart
Yes, Amber, I believe this is only the start

"That's beautiful, Seth," she said, swallowing her tears and kissing him on the cheek. "Thank you."

"I can never write unless it comes straight from my heart, Amber."

"That's why I love your letters," she said.

"I can't write like that except to you. That's how I knew you were the one I was saving my kisses for."

He was about to give her one of those kisses when the door opened behind them. Ben came out and sat beside her.

"What'ya doing out here, sis?" he teased. "Oh, Seth. I didn't see you there."

Amber smiled at her brother. Even though he was being obnoxious at the moment, she knew it was out of love, and she wasn't looking forward to saying good-bye to him this afternoon.

"I'm really going to miss you," she said, partially teasing and partially serious.

"Hey, maybe I could stay, and Seth could take my place. I'm sure he'd get better grades than I would."

"Uh--no," she said, leaning into Seth's side. "I'll miss you, but not that much."

Ben appeared to approve of Seth, but she had seen that big-brother watchful eye several times yesterday. He had no problem letting Seth know what he expected.

"You're going to take care of her, right?"

"Yes, I will," Seth said seriously. "I can't imagine doing anything else."

"She radiates His light, you know."

Amber turned and looked into Seth's face. She didn't think she had told him about letting Ben read his poem. His expression confirmed it.

"Yeah, I think I read that somewhere," Seth said.

"She tells me everything, you know."

"Ben!" Amber interjected and attempted to shove him off the porch.

Seth laughed. "I guess so. I will be sure and keep that in mind."

"I'm sure you will," Ben said. "I'm just having a little trouble thinking of her as being sixteen."

Her parents saved her from this embarrassing conversation. Once they were on their way to the van, Amber whispered an apology to Seth. But Seth wouldn't accept it.

"I know exactly how he feels, Amber. I have a sister too."

She hadn't thought of that and supposed she should be grateful to have a brother who was watching out for her. After church they went out for a family lunch, and Amber began to dread saying good-bye to her brother once they returned home. He'd gone away to camp the last three summers, but this felt different. Hugging Ben in the driveway at two-thirty, she clung to him tightly and let the tears fall.

"I'll be back to pester you at least once a month," he said.

She smiled but didn't let go.

"And I can see you're not going to be too lonely without me around. Mom and Dad didn't take my suggestion of keeping you locked in your room until you're twenty."

"I love you, Benny," she said. "Don't worry, okay? Jesus is taking good care of me."

"I know He is, sis. And He'd better be since that's what I've been praying for."

She laughed and stepped back, wiping her wet cheeks with her fingertips. Her mom and dad took their turns saying good-bye, and Amber went to go stand with Seth. Leaning into his chest, she was surprised when he tilted her chin up, wiped away a tear with his thumb, and gave her a sweet kiss. Even though her parents were focused on Ben, they were standing close by.

He did the same thing later when they were back in the house, kissing her briefly but tenderly after turning to say something to her while they were watching a movie with her parents. She didn't mind but felt surprised he would be so bold. Before today he had only kissed her when they were alone.

She probably wouldn't have said anything about it except by the time he needed to leave and she walked him out to say good-bye, he had done so three more times. Once more during the movie; once in the kitchen when they were making a banana-split to share and her mom was making one for herself and Daddy; and again when he was getting ready to leave and she took a book over to him he'd left on the kitchen table. That time he was in the middle of talking to her dad but averted his attention for a moment to thank her with more than words.

"I'm sorry, does that bother you?" he asked before they said their good-byes.

"No, I'm just surprised. Especially after Ben interrogated you this morning."

"We don't have anything to hide, Amber. If I only kiss you when we're alone, then it's like I do or I'm embarrassed about showing you how I feel. But I shouldn't be, and I'm not."

He kissed her sweetly once and then lingered longer the second time. "I will save those for when it's just you and me though."

She smiled at him. "Thanks again for the poem. I've been thinking about it all day."

He drew her close to him and held her gently. "And I'll be thinking of you all week."

"I checked the volleyball schedule, and we'll be at St. Mary's this Thursday if you want to come."

"I'll be there," he said, referring to one of the schools they played that was actually in Portland. It would be better for him than having to come all the way out here for their home game on Tuesday.

"I can't wait," she said.

"Will you keep dancing with me, Amber?"

"Yes."

"This is just the beginning, sweetheart."

"I know."

He kissed her one last time. She cherished the tenderness of his touch and the closeness she was becoming more and more used to between them.

"See you on Thursday," he whispered.

"Okay."

Chapter Sixteen

Amber saved her tears until after Seth was gone. Going to sit on the steps, she didn't try to wipe them away when her mom came out to sit beside her. She turned and cried on her shoulder.

"I didn't think it was possible to miss someone so much," she said after she'd calmed down a little. "And it's not like he's going to be gone for weeks and weeks like Ben."

"That doesn't matter when you feel the way you do about him."

"So you don't think I'm a mess?"

Her mom laughed. "Oh, I know you're a mess, Ammie. But with good reason."

She smiled and took the tissue her mother offered her. "I can't believe this is happening to me, Mom. I can't believe he feels the same way about me as I do about him."

"Believe it, sweetie. If you don't, you're going to miss out on something wonderful."

After her mom went back inside, she saw her Bible sitting on the porch swing. She'd left it there after she and Seth had done their reading from First John together, and she moved to the swing to take the poem from inside the front cover. Other than this morning when Seth had given it to her, she hadn't read it, but she wanted to, especially now.

She cherished the words once again, reading the entire poem twice and her favorite verse a third time:

And so we will dance, my jewel, my treasure
Not with meaningless talk and mere fleeting pleasure
But by seeking things above: His love and His heart
Yes, Amber, I believe this is only the start

At the bottom she saw Seth had written a verse reference she remembered seeing earlier but she hadn't looked up yet. Picking up her Bible, she turned to Jeremiah 29:13 and read it: *"You will seek me and find me when you seek me with all your heart."*

She took her journal and wrote the words at the top of a blank page, feeling chills go through her as she realized the words were spoken by God Himself and the amazing promise they contained. God didn't say He *might* be found. He said, 'You *will* find me.'

I want to seek you with all of my heart, God, and I claim your promise that I will find you. I remember Pastor Cooke talking about the same thing this morning during his message. He read those verses that say, 'Seek and you will find, ask and it will be given, knock and the door will be opened.' At the time I was thinking, 'Okay what can I ask God for?' And my thoughts were pretty small--a good volleyball season, good grades this semester, more time with Seth. What I should be asking for is more of you, right? I'm starting to get it! The more I have of you, the deeper you take me, and the more I have of everything I need, because all of that is found in you!

Thank you for Seth and his seeking heart. I ask for your blessing upon us. To be honest I'm not sure how to pray right now. I feel overwhelmed by this. You have brought me to this point in my life, and I'm thrilled and scared and excited about where you will take us from here. Help me to cling to you, and help me to give everything I have to give to my relationship with Seth. I don't have a clue what I'm doing! Am I really the girl he wants? How can that be?

Amber stopped writing and looked up when she heard a car coming up the driveway. It only took a second to realize it was Seth. Her heart leapt and so did she--right off the swing and down the steps to meet him when he pulled the car to a stop and got out.

"I needed to get gas and realized I'd forgotten my wallet," he said.

"Oh, that's too bad," she said with a smile. "What a bummer for you to have to come all the way back."

"Yeah, I'm really kicking myself," he said, pulling her close and kissing her playfully. "I could be halfway home by now, but instead I'm back here again."

Their sweet kissing was interrupted by her dad coming out the front door. He had Seth's wallet and held it up in the air. "Forget something, Seth?"

He stepped away from her and went to get it. Taking the wallet from her dad's hand, he said something Amber couldn't hear. Her dad laughed and glanced over Seth's shoulder, making eye contact with her and then shifting his eyes back to Seth and saying something else she couldn't hear.

After her dad disappeared back inside and Seth returned to her, she asked what they had been talking about, but he wouldn't tell her.

"Keeping secrets from me?" she said, putting her hands on her hips.

He smiled, reached for her elbow, and gently pulled her close to him. "I've got lots of good secrets," he said.

She laughed and put her arms around his neck. "Oh yeah? Like what?"

Seth stroked her arms lightly and laid his forehead against hers. "Like if I tell you they won't be secrets anymore."

"Come on, just one. Please?"

"Okay, just one."

She smiled and waited.

"I have a special surprise planned for you in a few weeks."

"What kind of surprise?"

"Nope. That would be two."

She faked a pout. He kissed it into a smile.

"I guess I can wait," she said, laughing as he started tickling her.

"Always keep them guessing," he said. "That's my motto."

"Them?"

"You know, all my girlfriends."

"Oh really? And how many would that be?"

"Mmmm, just one."

"Lucky girl."

"Luck has nothing to do with it. She drew me in with her beautiful smile and heart for God like a bug to a flame."

"Funny, my boyfriend did the same thing to me."

"Maybe we should get them together and then you and I can go out sometime."

"Yeah, maybe," she said. "Are you a good kisser?"

"Is he?"

"Yes. Is she?"

"Absolutely," he whispered and kissed her tenderly. "I get to see her on Thursday. I can't wait."

"I bet she can't either."

"That's what she tells me. But for the life of me, I can't figure out why."

She smiled. "I think it's the kisses."

"Yeah, I think you're right. I can't imagine what else it would be."

She kissed him gently and hugged him tight. "It's everything, Seth. I hope she means as much to you as you do to her."

"She does," he said, holding her close and letting out a huge sigh. "I promise you she does."

I'd love to hear how God has used
this story to touch your heart.

Write me at:

living_loved@yahoo.com

Titles in the Seeking Heart Series:

Made in the USA
Lexington, KY
25 March 2015